A Little Bush Maid

A Little Bush Maid

MARY GRANT BRUCE

BILLABONG BOOK ONE

Angus&Robertson

An imprint of HarperCollins*Publishers*

Angus&Robertson

An imprint of HarperCollins*Publishers*, Australia

First published in 1910 by Ward Lock, Melbourne and London
A&R revised edition with Afterword by Barbara Ker Wilson first published in 1992
Reprinted in 1993, 1994
This edition published in 1996
by HarperCollins*Publishers* Pty Limited
ACN 009 913 517
A member of the HarperCollins*Publishers* (Australia) Pty Limited Group

HarperCollins*Publishers*
25 Ryde Road, Pymble, Sydney, NSW 2073, Australia
31 View Road, Glenfield, Auckland 10, New Zealand
77–85 Fulham Palace Road, London W6 8JB, United Kingdom
Hazelton Lanes, 55 Avenue Road, Suite 2900, Toronto, Ontario M5R 3L2
and 1995 Markham Road, Scarborough, Ontario M1B 5M8, Canada
10 East 53rd Street, New York NY 10032, USA

National Library of Australia Cataloguing-in-Publication data:

Bruce, Mary Grant, 1878-1958.
   A little bush maid.
   ISBN 0 207 19104 2 (pbk.).
   ISBN 0 207 18586 7 (deluxe).
   I. Title. (Series : Bruce, Mary Grant, 1878-1958. Billabong : bk. 1).
A823.2

Printed by Australian Print Group, Sydney
5 4 3 2 1
99 98 97 96

Contents

CHAPTER 1

Billabong

NORAH'S home was on a big station in the north of Victoria — so large that you could almost, in her own phrase, "ride all day and never see anyone you didn't want to see"; which was a great advantage in Norah's eyes. Not that Billabong Station ever seemed to the little girl a place that you needed to praise in any way. It occupied so very modest a position as the loveliest part of the world!

The homestead was built on a gentle rise that sloped gradually away on every side; in front to the wide plain, dotted with huge gum trees and great grey box groves, and at the back, after you had passed through the well-kept vegetable garden and orchard, to a long lagoon, bordered with trees and fringed with tall bulrushes and waving reeds.

The house itself was old and quaint and rambling, part of the old wattle and daub walls yet remaining in some of the outhouses, as well as the grey shingle roof. There was a more modern part, for the house had been added to from time to time by different owners, though no additions had been made since Norah's father brought home his young wife, fifteen years before this story opens. Then he had built a large new wing with wide and lofty rooms, and round all had put a very broad, tiled verandah. The creepers had had time to twine round thin massive posts in those fifteen years, and some even lay in great masses on the verandah roof; tecoma, pink and salmon-coloured; purple bougainvillea, and the snowy mandevillea clusters. Hard-headed people said this was not good for the building — but Norah's mother had planted them, and because she had loved them they were never touched.

There was a huge front garden, not at all a proper kind of garden, but a great stretch of smooth buffalo grass, dotted with all kinds of trees, amongst which flower beds cropped up in most unexpected and unlikely places, just as if some giant had flung them out on the grass like a handful of pebbles that scattered as they flew. They were always trim and tidy, and the gardener, Hogg, was terribly strict, and woe betide the author of any small footmarks that he found on one of the freshly raked surfaces. Nothing annoyed him more than the odd bulbs that used to come up in the midst of his precious buffalo grass; impertinent crocuses and daffodils and hyacinths, that certainly had no right there. "Blest if I know how they ever gets there!" Hogg would say, scratching his head. Whereat Norah was wont to retire behind a pyramid tree for purposes of mirth.

Hogg's sworn foe was Lee Wing, the Chinese gardener, who reigned supreme in the orchard and kingdom of vegetables — not quite the same thing as the vegetable kingdom, by the way.

Lee Wing was very fat, his broad, yellow face

generally wearing a cheerful grin — unless he happened to catch sigh of Hogg. His long pigtail was always concealed under his flapping straw hat. Once Jim, who was Norah's big brother, had found him asleep in his hut with the pigtail drooping over the edge of the bunk. Jim thought the opportunity too good to lose and, with such deftness that the Chinese never stirred, he tied the end of the pigtail to the back of a chair — with rather startling results when Lee Wing awoke with a sudden sense of being late, and made a spring from the bunk. The chair of course followed him, and the loud yell of fear and pain raised by the victim brought half the homestead to the scene of the catastrophe. Jim was the only one who did not wait for developments. He found business at the lagoon.

The queerest part of it was that Lee Wing firmly believed Hogg to be the author of his woe. Nothing moved him from this view, not even when Jim, finding how matters stood, owned up like a man. "You allee same goo' boy," said the pigtailed one, proffering him a succulent raw turnip. "Me know. You tellee fine large crammee. Hogg, he tellee crammee, too. So dly up!" And Jim, finding expostulation useless, "dried up" accordingly and ate the turnip.

To the right of the homestead at Billabong a clump of box trees sheltered the stables that were the unspoken pride of Mr. Linton's heart.

Before his time the stables had been a conglomerate mass, bark-roofed, slab-sided, falling to decay; added to as each successive owner had thought fit, with a final mixture of old and new

that was neither convenient nor beautiful. Mr.
Linton had apologised to his horses during his first
week of occupancy and, in the second, turning
them out to grass with less apology, had pulled
down the ricketty old sheds, replacing them with
a compact and handsome building of red brick,
with room for half a dozen buggies, men's
quarters, harness and feed rooms, many loose
boxes and a loft where a ball could have been held
— and where, indeed, many a one was held, when
all the young farmers and stockmen and shearers
from far and near brought each his lass and
tripped it from early night to early dawn, to the
strains of old Andy Ferguson's fiddle and young
Dave Boone's concertina. Norah had been allowed
to look on at one or two of these gatherings. She
thought them the height of human bliss, and was
only sorry that sheer inability to dance prevented
her from "taking the floor" with Mick Shanahan,
the horse breaker, who had paid her the
compliment of asking her first. It was a great
compliment, too, Norah felt, seeing what a man of
agility and splendid accomplishments was Mick —
and that she was only nine.

There was one loose box which was Norah's very
own property, and without her permission no
horse was ever put in it except its rightful
occupant — Bobs, whose name was proudly
displayed over the door in Jim's best carving.

Bobs had always belonged to Norah. He had
been given to her as a foal, when Norah used to
ride a round little black sheltie, as easy to fall off
as to mount. He was a beauty even then, Norah
thought; and her father had looked approvingly at

the long-legged baby, with his fine, well-bred head.
"You will have something worth riding when that
fellow is fit to break in, my girlie," he had said,
and his prophecy had been amply fulfilled. Mick
Shanahan said he'd never put a leg over a finer
pony. Norah knew there never had been a finer
anywhere. He was a big pony, very dark bay in
colour, and "as handsome as paint," and with the
kindest disposition; full of life and "go," but
without the smallest particle of vice. It was an
even question which loved the other best, Bobs or
Norah. No one ever rode him except his little
mistress. The pair were hard to beat — so the men
said.

To Norah the stables were the heart of
Billabong. The house was all very well — of course
she loved it; and she loved her own little room,
with its red carpet and dainty white furniture, and
the two long windows that looked out over the
green plain. That was all right; so were the garden
and the big orchard — especially in summer time!
The only part that was not "all right" was the
drawing-room — an apartment of gloomy,
seldom-used splendour that Norah hated with her
whole heart.

But the stables were an abiding refuge. She was
never dull there. Apart from the never-failing
welcome in Bobs' loose box, there was the dim,
fragrant loft, where the sunbeams only managed
to send dusty rays of light across the gloom. Here
Norah used to lie on the sweet hay and think
tremendous thoughts; here also she laid deep
plans for catching rats — and caught scores in
traps of her own devising. Norah hated rats, but

nothing could induce her to wage war against the mice. "Poor little chaps!" she said, "they're so little — and — and soft!" And she was quite saddened if by chance she found a stray mouse in any of her shrewdly designed traps for the benefit of the larger game which infested the stables and had even the hardihood to annoy Bobs!

Norah had never known her mother. She was only a tiny baby when that young mother died — a sudden, terrible blow, that changed her father in a night from a young man to an old one. It was nearly eleven years ago now, but no one ever dared to speak to David Linton of his wife. Sometimes Norah used to ask Jim about her mother — Jim was fifteen, and could remember just a little; but his memories were so vague and misty that his information was unsatisfactory. And, after all, Norah did not trouble much. She had always been so happy that she could not imagine that to have had a mother would have made any particular difference to her happiness. You see, she did not know.

She had grown just as the bush wild flowers grow — hardy, unchecked, almost untended; for, though old Nurse had always been there, her nurseling had gone her own way from the time she could toddle. She was everybody's pet and plaything; the only being who had power to make her stern, silent father smile — almost the only one who ever saw the softer side of his character. He was fond and proud of Jim — glad that the boy was growing up straight and strong and manly, able to make his way in the world. But Norah was his heart's desire.

Of course she was spoilt — if spoiling consists in rarely checking an impulse. All her life Norah had done pretty well whatever she wanted — which meant that she had lived out of doors, followed in Jim's footsteps wherever practicable (and in a good many ways most people would have thought distinctly impracticable), and spent about two-thirds of her waking time on horseback. But the spoiling was not of a very harmful kind. Her chosen pursuits brought her under the unspoken discipline of the work of the station, wherein ordinary instinct taught her to do as others did, and conform to their ways. She had all the dread of being thought "silly" that marks the girl who imitates boyish ways. Jim's rare growl, "Have a little sense!" went farther home than a whole volume of admonitions of a more ordinarily genuine feminine type.

She had no little girlfriends, for none was nearer than the nearest township — Cunjee, seventeen miles away. Moreover, little girls bored Norah frightfully. They seemed a species quite distinct from herself. They prattled of dolls; they loved to skip, to dress up and "play ladies"; and when Norah spoke of the superior joys of cutting out cattle or coursing hares over the Long Plain, they stared at her with blank lack of understanding. With boys she got on much better. Jim and she were tremendous chums, and she had moped sadly when he went to Melbourne to school. Holidays then became the shining events of the year, and the boys whom Jim brought home with him, at first prone to look down on the small girl with lofty condescension, generally ended by

voting her "no end of a jolly kid," and according
her the respect due to a person who could teach
them more of bush life than they had dreamed of.

But Norah's principal mate was her father. Day
after day they were together, riding over the run,
working the cattle, walking through the thick
scrub of the backwater, driving young, half-
broken horses in the high dog-cart to Cunjee —
they were rarely apart. David Linton seldom
made a plan that did not naturally include Norah.
She was a wise little companion, too; ready
enough to chatter like a magpie if her father were
in the mood, but quick to note if he were not, and
then quite content to be silently beside him,
perhaps for hours. They understood each other
perfectly. Norah never could make out the people
who pitied her for having no friends of her own
age. How could she possibly be bothered with
children, she reflected, when she had Daddy?

As for Norah's education, that was of the kind
best defined as a minus quantity.

"I won't have her bothered with books too early,"
Mr. Linton had said when Nurse hinted, on
Norah's eighth birthday, that it was time she
began the rudiments of learning. "Time enough yet
— we don't want to make a bookworm of her!"

Whereat Nurse smiled demurely, knowing that
that was the last thing to be afraid of in connexion
with her child. But she worried in her responsible
old soul all the same; and when a wet day or the
occasional absence of Mr. Linton left Norah
without occupation, she induced her to begin a few
elementary lessons. The child was quick enough,
and soon learned to read fairly well and to write

laboriously; but there Nurse's teaching from books ended.

Of other and practical teaching, however, she had a greater store. Mr. Linton had a strong leaning towards the old-fashioned virtues, and it was at a word from him that Norah had gone to the kitchen and asked Mrs. Brown to teach her to cook. Mrs. Brown — fat, good-natured and adoring — was all acquiescence, and by the time Norah was eleven she knew more of cooking and general housekeeping than many girls grown up and fancying themselves ready to undertake houses of their own. Moreover, she could sew rather well, though she frankly detested the accomplishment. The one form of work she cared for was knitting, and it was her boast that her father wore only the socks she manufactured for him.

Norah's one gentle passion was music. She had inherited from her mother a natural instinct and an absolutely true ear, and before she was seven she could strum on the old piano in a way very satisfying to herself and awe-inspiring to the admiring nurse. Her talent increased yearly, and at ten she could play anything she heard — from ear, for she had never been taught a note of music. It was, indeed, her growing capabilities in this respect that forced upon her father the need for proper tuition for the child. However, a stopgap was found in the person of the book-keeper, a young Englishman, who knew more of music than accounts. He readily undertook Norah's instruction, and the lessons bore moderately good effect — the moderation being due to a not unnatural disinclination on the pupil's part to

walk where she had been accustomed to run, and
to a fixed loathing to practise. As the latter
necessary, if uninteresting, pursuit was left
entirely to her own discretion — for one ever
dreamed of ordering Norah to the piano — it is
small wonder if it suffered beside the superior
attractions of riding Bobs, rat trapping, "shinning
up" trees, fishing in the lagoon and generally
disporting herself as a maiden may whom
conventional restrictions have never trammelled.

It follows that the music lessons, twice a week,
were times of woe for Mr. Groom, the teacher. He
was an earnest young man, with a sincere desire
for his pupil's improvement, and it was certainly
disheartening to find on Friday that the words of
Tuesday had apparently gone in at one ear and
out at the other simultaneously. Sometimes he
would remonstrate.

"You haven't got on with that piece a bit!"

"What's the good?" the pupil would remark,
twisting round on the music stool. "I can play
nearly all of it from ear!"

"That's not the same" — severely — "that's only
frivolling. I'm not here to teach you to strum."

"No," Norah would agree abstractedly. "Mr.
Groom, you know that poley bullock down in the
far end paddock —"

"No, I don't," severely. "This is a music lesson,
Norah; you're not after cattle now!"

"Wish I were!" sighed the pupil. "Well, will you
come out with the dogs this afternoon?"

"Can't; I'm wanted in the office. Now, Norah —"

"But if I asked father to spare you?"

"Oh, I'd like to right enough." Mr. Groom was

young, and the temptress, if younger, was skilled in wiles. "But your father —"

"Oh, I can manage Dad. I'll go and see him now." She would be at the door before her teacher perceived that his opportunity was vanishing.

"Norah, come back! If I'm to go out, you must play this first — and get it right."

Mr. Groom could be firm on occasions. "Come along, you little shirker!" and Norah would unwillingly return to the music stool, and worry laboriously through a page of the hated Czerny.

CHAPTER 2

Pets and Playthings

AFTER her father, Norah's chief companions were her pets.

These were a numerous and varied band, and required no small amount of attention. Bobs, of course, came first — no other animal could possibly approach him in favour. But after Bobs came a long procession, beginning with Tait, the collie, and ending with the last brood of fluffy Orpington chicks, or perhaps the newest thing in disabled birds, picked up, fluttering and helpless, in the yard or orchard. There was room in Norah's heart for them all.

Tait was a beauty — a rough-haired collie, with a splendid head, and big, faithful brown eyes, that spoke more eloquently than many persons' tongues. He was, like most of the breed, ready to be friends with anyone; but his little mistress was dearest of all, and he worshipped her with abject devotion. Norah never went anywhere without him; Tait saw to that. He seemed always on the watch for her coming, and she was never more than a few yards from the house before the big dog was silently brushing the grass by her side. His greatest joy was to follow her on long rides into the bush, putting up an occasional hare and scurrying after it in the futile way of collies, barking at the swallows overhead, and keeping pace with Bobs' long, easy canter.

Puck used to come on these excursions too. He was the only being for whom it was suspected that Tait felt a mild dislike — an impudent Irish terrier, full of fun and mischief, yet with a somewhat unfriendly and suspicious temperament that made him, perhaps, a better guardian for Norah than the benevolently disposed Tait. Puck had a nasty, inquiring mind — an unpleasant way of sniffing round the legs of tramps that generally induced those gentry to find the top rail of fence a more calm and more desirable spot than the level of the ground. Indian hawkers feared him and hated him in equal measure. He could bite, and occasionally did bite, his victims being always selected with judgment and discretion, generally vagrants emboldened to insolence by seeing no men about the kitchen when all hands were out mustering or busy on the run. When Puck bit, it was with no uncertain tooth. He was suspected of a desire to taste the blood of everyone who went near Norah, though his cannibalistic propensities were curbed by stern discipline.

Only once had he had anything like a free hand — or a free tooth.

Norah was out riding, a good way from the homestead, when a particularly unpleasant-looking fellow accosted her, and asked for money. Norah stared.

"I haven't got any," she said. "Anyhow, Father doesn't let us give away money to travellers — only tucker."

"Oh, doesn't he?" the fellow said unpleasantly. "Well, I want money, not grub." He laid a compelling hand on Bobs' bridle as Norah tried to pass him. "Come," he said, "that bracelet'll do!"

It was a pretty little gold watch set in a leather bangle — father's birthday present, only a few weeks old. Norah simply laughed — she scarcely comprehended so amazing a thing as that this man should really intend to rob her.

"Get out of my way," she said. "You can't have that!"

"Can't I!" He caught her wrist. "Give it quietly now, or I'll —"

The sentence was not completed. A yellow streak hurled itself through the air, as Puck, who had been investigating a tussock for lizards, awoke to the situation. Something like a vice gripped the swagman by the leg, and he dropped Norah's wrist and bridle and roared like any bull. The "something" hung on fiercely, silently, and the victim hopped and raved and begged for mercy.

Norah had ridden a little way on. She called softly to Puck.

"Here, boy!"

Puck did not relinquish his grip. He looked pleadingly at his little mistress across the swagman's trouser-leg. Norah struck her saddle sharply with her whip.

"Here, sir! — drop it!"

Puck dropped it reluctantly, and came across to

Bobs, his head hanging. The swagman sat down
on the ground and nursed his leg.

"That served you right!" Norah said with
judicial severity. "You hadn't any business to grab
my watch. Now, if you'll go up to the house they'll
give you some tucker and a rag for your leg!"

She rode off, whistling to Puck. The swagman
gaped and muttered various remarks. He did not
call at the house.

Norah was supposed to manage the fowls, but
her management was almost entirely ornamental,
and it is to be feared that the poultry yard would
have fared but poorly had it depended upon her
alone. All the fowls were hers. She said so, and
no one contradicted her. Still, whenever one was
wanted for the table, it was ruthlessly slain. And
it was black Billy who fed them night and
morning, and Mrs. Brown who gathered the eggs,
and saw that the houses were safely shut against
the foxes every evening. Norah's chief part in the
management lay in looking after the setting hens.
At first she firmly checked their broody instincts
by shutting them callously under boxes, despite
pecks and loud protests. Later, when their mood
refused to change, she loved to prepare them soft
nests in boxes, and to imprison them there until
they took kindly to their seclusion. Then it was
hard work to wait three weeks until the first fluffy
heads peeped out from the angry mother's wing,
after which Norah was a blissfully adoring
caretaker until the downy balls began to get
ragged, as the first wing and tail feathers showed.
Then the chicks became uninteresting, and were
handed over to black Billy.

Besides her own pets there were Jim's.

"Mind, they're in your care," Jim had said sternly, on the evening before his departure for school. They were making a tour of the place — Jim outwardly very cheerful and unconcerned, Norah plunged in woe. She did not attempt to conceal it. She had taken Jim's arm, and it was sufficient proof of his state of mind that he did not shake it off. Indeed, the indications were that he was glad of the loving little hand tucked into the bend of his arm.

"Yes, Jim; I'll look after them."

"I don't want you to bother feeding them yourself," Jim said magnanimously. "That 'ud be rather too much of a contract for a kid, wouldn't it? Only keep an eye on 'em, and round up Billy if he doesn't do his work. He's a terror if he shirks, and unless you watch him like a cat he'll never change the water in the tins every morning. Lots of times I've had to do it myself!"

"I'd do it myself soon'n let them go without, Jim, dear," said the small voice, with a suspicion of a choke.

"Don't you do it," said Jim. "Just see that Billy does it. It is his job, after all. I only want you to go round 'em every day, and see that they're all right."

So daily Norah used to make her pilgrimage round Jim's pets. There were the guinea pigs — a rapidly increasing band, in an enclosure specially built for them by Jim — a light frame, netted carefully everywhere, and so constructed that it could be moved from place to place, giving them a fresh grass run continually. Then there

were two young wallabies and a little brush
kangaroo, which lived in a little paddock all their
own, and were as tame as kittens. Norah loved
this trio especially, and always had a game with
them on her daily visit. There was a shy
gentleman which Norah called a tortoise, because
she never could remember if he were a turtle or
a tortoise. He lived in a small enclosure, with a
tiny water hole, and his disposition was extremely
retiring. In private Norah did not feel drawn to
this member of her charge, but she paid him
double attention, from an inward feeling of guilt,
and because Jim set a high value upon him.

"He's such a wise old chap," Jim would say.
"Nobody knows what he's thinking of!"

In her heart of hearts Norah did not believe that
mattered very much.

But when the stables had been visited and Bobs
and Sirdar (Jim's neglected pony) interviewed;
when Tait and Puck had had their breakfast
bones; when wallabies and kangaroo had been
inspected (with a critical eye to their water tins),
and the turtle had impassively received a
praiseworthy attempt to draw him out; when the
chicks had all been fed, and the guinea pigs
(unlike the leopard) had changed their spot for the
day — there still remained the birds.

The birds were a colony in themselves. There
was a big aviary, large enough for little trees and
big shrubs to grow in, where a happy family lived
whose members included several kinds of
honey-eaters, Queensland finches, blackbirds and
a dozen other tiny shy things which flitted quickly
from bush to bush all day. They knew Norah and,

when she entered their home, would flutter down
and perch on her head and shoulders, and look
inquisitively for the flowers she always brought
them. Sometimes Norah would wear some
artificial flowers, by way of a joke. It was funny
to see the little honey-eaters thrusting in their
long beaks again and again in search of the sweet
drops they had learned to expect in flowers, and
funnier still to watch the air of disgust with which
they would give up the attempt.

There were doves everywhere — not in cages,
for they never tried to escape. Their soft "coo"
murmured drowsily all around. There were
pigeons, too, in a most elaborate pigeon cote —
another effort of Jim's carpentering skill. These
were as tame as the smaller birds, and on Norah's
appearance would swoop down upon her in a
cloud. They had done so once when she was
mounted on Bobs, to the pony's very great alarm
and disgust. He took to his heels promptly. "I don't
think he stopped for two miles!" Norah said. Since
then, however, Bobs had grown used to the
pigeons fluttering and circling round him. It was
a pretty sight to watch them all together, child
and pony half hidden beneath their load of birds.

The canaries had a cage to themselves — a very
smart one, with every device for making canary
life endurable in captivity. Certainly Norah's birds
seemed happy enough, and the sweet songs of the
canaries were delightful. I think they were
Norah's favourites amongst her feathered flock.

Finally there were two talkative members —
Fudge the parrot, and old Caesar, a very fine
white cockatoo. Fudge had been caught young, and

his education had been of a liberal order. An apt
pupil, he had picked up various items of
knowledge, and had blended them into a whole
that was scarcely harmonious. Bits of slang
learned from Jim and the stockmen were mingled
with fragments of hymns warbled by Mrs. Brown
and sharp curt orders delivered to dogs. A French
swagman, who had hurt his foot and been obliged
to camp for a few days at the homestead, supplied
Fudge with several Parisian remarks that were
very effective. Every member of the household had
tried to teach him to whistle some special tune.
Unfortunately, the lessons had been delivered at
the same time, and the result was the most
amazing jumble of melody, which Fudge delivered
with an air of deepest satisfaction. As Jim said,
"You never know if he's whistling 'God Save the
King,' 'Pop Goes the Weasel,' or 'The Wearin' o'
the Green,' but it doesn't make any difference to
Fudge's enjoyment!"

Caesar was a giant among cockatoos, and had
a full sense of his own importance.

He had been shot when very young, some stray
pellets having found their way into his wing.
Norah had found him fluttering helplessly along
the ground, and had picked him up, sustaining a
severe peck in doing so. It was, however, the first
and last peck he ever gave Norah. From that
moment he seemed to recognise her as a friend,
and to adopt her as an intimate — marks of
esteem he accorded to very few others. Norah had
handed him to Jim on arriving at the house, a
change which the bird resented by a savage attack
on Jim's thumb. Jim was no hero — at the age of

eleven. He dropped the cockatoo like a hot coal. "Great Caesar!" he exclaimed, sucking his thumb, and Caesar he was christened in that moment.

After his recovery, which was a long and tedious process, Caesar showed no inclination to leave the homestead. He used to strut about the back yard, and frequent the kitchen door, very much after the fashion of a house-dog. He was, indeed, as valuable as a watch-dog, for the appearance of any stranger was the signal for a volley of shrieks and chatter, sufficient to alarm any household. However, Caesar's liberty had to be restricted, for he became somewhat of a menace to all he did not choose to care for, and his attacks on the ankles were no joking matter.

To the dogs he was a constant terror. He hated all alike, and would "go for" big Tait as readily as for cheerful little Puck, and not a dog on the place would face him. So at last a stand and a chain were bought for Caesar, and on his perch he lived in solitary splendour, while his enemies took good care to keep beyond his reach. Norah he always loved, and those whom he had managed to bite — their number was large — used to experience thrills on seeing the little girl hold him close to her face while he rubbed his beak up and down her cheek. He tolerated black Billy, who fed him, and was respectful to Mr. Linton; but he worshipped Mrs. Brown, the cook, and her appearance at the kitchen door, which he could see from his stand, caused an instant outbreak of cheers and chatter, varied by touching appeals to "scratch Cocky." His chief foe was Mrs. Brown's big yellow cat, who not only dared to share the adored one's affections, but was openly aggressive at times, and loved to steal the cockatoo's food.

Caesar, on his perch, apparently wrapped in dreamless slumber, would in reality be watching the stealthy movements of Tim, the cat, who would come scouting through the grass towards the tin of food. Just out of reach, Tim would lie down and feign sleep as deep as Caesar's, though every muscle in his body was tense with readiness for the sudden spring. So they would remain, perhaps many minutes. Tim's patience never gave out. Sometimes Caesar's would, and he would open his eyes and flap round on his perch, shouting much bad bird language at the retreating Tim. But more often both remained motionless until the cat sprang suddenly at the food tin. More often than not he was too quick for Caesar, and would drag the tin beyond reach of the chain before the bird could defend it, in which case the wrath of the defeated was awful to behold. But sometimes Caesar managed to anticipate the leap, and Tim did not readily forget those distressful moments when the cockatoo had him by the fur with beak and claw. He would escape, showing several patches where his coat had been torn, and remained in a state of dejection for two or three days, during which battles were discontinued. It took Caesar almost as long to recover from the wild state of triumph into which his rare victories threw him.

CHAPTER 3

A Menagerie Race

THE first time that Jim returned from school was for the Easter holidays.

He brought a couple of mates with him — boys from New South Wales and Queensland, Harry Trevor and Walter Meadows. Harry was a little older than Jim — a short, thick-set lad, very fair and solemn, with expressionless grey eyes, looking out beneath a shock of flaxen hair. Those who knew him not said that he was stupid. Those who knew him said that you couldn't tell old Harry much that he didn't know. Those who knew him very well said that you could depend on Trevor to his last gasp. Jim loved him — and there were few people Jim loved.

Walter — or Wally — Meadows was a different type; long and thin for fourteen, burnt to almost African darkness; a wag of a boy, with merry brown eyes, and a temperament unable to be depressed for more than five minutes at a time. He was always in scrapes at school, but a great favourite with masters and boys notwithstanding; and he straightway laid his boyish heart down at

Norah's feet, and was her slave from the first day they met.

Norah like them both. She had been desperately afraid that they would try to take Jim away from her, and was much relieved to find that they welcomed her cheerfully into their plans. They were good riders, and the four had splendid gallops over the plains after hares. Also they admired Bobs fervently, and that was always a passport to Norah's heart.

It was on the third day of their visit, and they were making the morning round of the pets, when a brilliant idea came to Wally.

"Let's have a menagerie race!" he cried suddenly.

"What's that?" Norah asked blankly.

"Why, you each drive an animal," explained Wally, the words tumbling over one another in his haste. "Say you drive the kangaroo, 'n me the wallabies, 'n Jim the Orpington rooster, 'n we'll give old Harry the tortoise — turloise, I beg pardon!"

"Thanks," said Harry drily. "The tortoise scored once, you know, young Wally!"

"Well, old man, you take him," Wally said kindly. "Wouldn't stand in your way for a moment. We can use harness, can't we?"

"Don't know," Jim said. "I never studied the rules of menagerie racing. Use bridles, anyhow. It's a good idea, I think. Let's see how many starters we can muster."

They cruised round. Dogs were barred as being too intelligent — horses were, of course, out of the question. Finally they fixed on the possible candidates. They were the kangaroo, the wallabies, a big black Orpington "rooster," Fudge the parrot, Caesar the cockatoo, Mrs. Brown's big yellow cat, Tim, and the "turloise."

"Eight," said Harry laconically. The starters were all mustered in one enclosure, and were on the worse of terms. "We'll need more jockeys — if you call 'em jockeys."

"Well, there's black Billy," Jim said, "he's available, and he'll drive whichever he's told, and that's a comfort. That's five. And we'll rouse out old Lee Wing, and Hogg, that's a ripping idea, 'cause they hate each other so. Seven. Who's eight? Oh, I know! We'll get Mrs. Brown."

Mrs. Brown was accordingly bearded in her den and, protesting vigorously that she had no mind for racing, haled forth into the open. She was a huge woman, as good-natured as she was fat, which said a good deal. In her print dress, with enormous white apron and flapping sun bonnet, she looked as unlikely a "jockey" as could be imagined.

Lee Wing, discovered in the onion bed, was presently brought to the scratch, despite his protests. He said he "couldn't lun," but was told that in all probability no running would be required of him. He also said "no can dlive" many times, and further remarked, "Allee same gleat bosh." When he saw his arch enemy Hogg among the competitors his resentment was keen, and Wally was told off to restrain him from flight.

Hogg was, as Jim put it, rooting amongst the roses, and grunted freely on his way to the post. He could never refuse Norah anything, but this proceeding was much beneath his dignity, and the sight of Lee Wing did not tend to improve his view of the matter. He stood aloof, with a cold, proud smile, like a hero of melodrama.

Black Billy was, of course, in the stables, and came with alacrity. He had not much English and that little was broken, but he worshipped the Linton children — Jim especially, and would obey him unquestioningly.

"All here?" asked Jim, looking round. "Five, six, eight — that's all serene. Now who's going to drive who?"

Opinions on that point were mixed. Everyone wanted the kangaroo, and at last a general vote gave him to Norah. Wally chose one wallaby. He said it was only natural, and made a further remark about the feelings of the others when "Wally and his wallaby should wallow by them" that was happily quenched by Harry, who adopted the simple plan of sitting on the orator. Harry secured the second wallaby, and black Billy was given the Orpington rooster as his steed. Mrs. Brown from the first applied for the tortoise. She said it meant less exertion, and she preferred to be slow and sure, without any risk of over-work. Hogg chose the yellow cat, Tim, and Lee Wing was given Caesar, the cockatoo.

"Leaving old Fudge for me," Jim said ruefully. "What sort of a chance do you think I've got? Never mind, I'm used to being suppressed."

"Good for you," observed Harry. "Now, how 'bout harness?"

"Well, we'll leave that to individual taste," Jim said. "Here's a ball of string, and there are plenty of light straps. Mrs. Brown — you're the leading lady. How shall I harness your prancing steed for you?"

"You will have your joke, Master Jim," retorted Mrs. Brown, bridling and beaming. "Now, I don't think I'll harness my poor beastie at all. Give me a couple of sticks to keep his head the right way and to poke him gently, and we'll beat you all yet!"

Norah and the two boys fixed up fearful and wonderful harness for their nominations — collars of straps, and long string headpieces and reins. The animals objected strongly to being harnessed, and the process was most entertaining. Mrs. Brown was particularly appreciative, and at length in a paroxysm of mirth narrowly escaped sitting down on the tortoise.

Black Billy's harness was not extensive. He tied a string round the black Orpington's leg, and retired to the stable for a few minutes, returning with a bulging pocket, the contents of which he did not communicate. Hogg did not attempt to bit and bridle the yellow cat, which was much annoyed at the whole proceeding. Instead he fixed up a collar and traces of string, and chose a long cane, more, he said, for purposes of defence than for anything else. Lee Wing and Jim harnessed their steeds in the same way — with a long string tied to each leg.

"All ready?" Jim queried. "Toe the line!"

The course was across a small paddock near the house — a distance of about thirty yards — and the competitors were ranged up with no little difficulty. Luckily, the line was a wide one, admitting of considerable space between each starter, or the send-off might have been inextricably confused. However, they were all arranged at last, and Jim, in a stentorian voice, gave the word to "Go."

As the signal was given, the drivers urged on their steeds according to their judgment, and with magnificent results.

First to get off the line were the wallabies and the kangaroo. They fled, each his several way, and after them went their drivers, in great haste. The kangaroo had all the best of the start. So remarkable was his bound that he twitched his reins quite out of Norah's hands, and made for the fence of the paddock. It was an open one, which let him through easily. The wallabies, seeing his shining success, followed his course, and midway managed to entangle their reins, at which Wally and Harry were wildly hauling. Confusion became disorder, and the wallabies at length reduced themselves to a tangle, out of which they had to be assisted by means of Harry's pocket knife.

Jim had no luck. The parrot went off well, but very soon seemed to regret his rashness and, despite all Jim's endeavours, returned with solemnity to the start, where he paused and talked fluently in the mixed language that was all his own. In desperation Jim tried to pull him along, but Fudge simply walked round and round him, until he had exhausted his driver's patience, and was "turned out."

The most spirited of the competitors were decidedly the cockatoo and Tim. They were panting for each other's blood from the start, and before they had been urged over a quarter of the

way they found an opportunity of warfare, and
seized it simultaneously. Then the air grew murky
with sound — cockatoo shrieks, mingled with cat
calls and fluent Chinese, cutting across Hogg's
good, broad Scots. Naturally, the strings of the
harness became fatally twisted immediately, and
soon the combatants were bound together with a
firmness which not all the efforts of their drivers
could undo. A sudden movement of the pair made
Lee Wing spring back hastily, whereupon he
tripped and stumbled violently against Hogg.

Hogg's temper was at vanishing point, and this
was the last straw.

"Ye pig-tailed image!" he exclaimed furiously.
Drawing back, he aimed a blow at Lee Wing,
which would have effectively put that gentle
Mongolian out of the race had he not dodged
quickly. He shouted something in his own
language, which was evidently of no compli-
mentary nature, and hurled himself like a yellow
tornado upon the angry Scotsman. They struck out
at each other with all possible ill-will, but their
science was much impeded by the fact that the cat
and cockatoo were fighting fiercely amongst their
legs. Finally Lee Wing tripped over Tim, and sat
down abruptly, receiving as he did so an
impassioned peck from Caesar which elicited from
him a loud yell of anguish. Hogg, attempting to
follow up his advantage, was checked suddenly by
Jim, who left his parrot to its own devices, and
arrived on the scene at full gallop.

"You are a blessed pair of duffers!" said Jim
wrathfully. "Look here, if father catches you
fighting there'll be the most awful row — and I'll

be in it, too, what's worse. Clear out, for goodness'
sake, before he comes along, and don't get in each
other's road again!" and each nursing bitterness
in his heart, the rival gardeners returned to their
respective beds of roses and onions.

Left to their own devices, the yellow cat and
cockatoo departed also, in a turmoil of wrath, with
far and feathers flying in equal proportions.
Eventually Tim found discretion the better part of
valour and scurried away to the safe shelter of the
kitchen, pursued by Caesar with loud shrieks of
defiance and victory — sounds of joyful triumph
which lasted long after he had regained his perch
and been securely fastened by the leg with his
hated chain.

Black Billy, meanwhile, had paid strict
attention to business. The vagaries of wallabies
and kangaroo, of cat and parrot and cockatoo, had
no attraction for the dusky leader of the big black
Orpington rooster.

The Orpington — Jonah, Norah called him —
was not inclined to race. He had tugged furiously
at his leg rope, with much outcry and indignation,
until Billy, finding himself alone, owing to the
eccentric behaviour of the other starters, had
resorted to different tactics by no means devoid of
native cunning. Slackening the line, he suddenly
produced from his pocket a few grains of wheat,
and spread them temptingly before Jonah.

Now Jonah was a tame bird. He was accustomed to being handled, and had only been indignant at the disgrace of bonds. This new departure
was something he understood; so he gobbled up

the wheat with alacrity, and looked up inquiringly
for more.

"Right oh!" said Billy, retiring a few steps down
the track and bringing out another grain. Jonah
sprang after it, and then was dazzled with the
view of two lying yet a few yards farther off. So,
feeding and coaxing, black Billy worked his
unsuspecting steed across the little paddock.

No one was near when he reached the winning
post, to which he promptly tied Jonah, and, his
purpose being accomplished, and no need of
further bribery being necessary, sat down beside
him and meditatively began to chew the
remainder of his wheat. Jonah looked indignant,
and poked round after more grains, an attention
which Billy met with jeers and continued heartless
mastication, until the deluded Orpington gave up
the question in disgust, and retired to the limit of
his tether. Billy sat quietly, with steadfast
glittering eyes twinkling in his dusky face.

"Hallo!" It was Jim's voice. "Where are all the
rest? D'you mean to say you're the only one to get
here?"

Billy grinned silently.

Sounds of mirth floated over the grass, and
Norah, Harry and Wally raced up.

"Where are your mokes?" queried Jim. "The
good knights are dust, Their mokes are rust,"
misquoted Wally cheerfully. "We don't know, bless
you. Cleared out, harness and all. We'll have a
wallaby and kangaroo hunt after this. Who's won?"

"Billy," said Jim, indicating that sable hero. "In
a common walk. Fed him over. All right, now,

Billy, you catch-um kangaroo, wallaby — d'you hear?"

Billy showed a set of amazingly white teeth in a broad grin, and departed swiftly and silently.

"Where's Lee Wing?"

"Had to tear him off Hogg!" Jim grinned. "You never saw such a shindy. They've retired in bad order."

"Where's Fudge?"

"Left at the post!"

"Where's Mrs. Brown — and the tortoise?"

"Great Scott!" Jim looked round blankly. "That never occurred to me. Where is she, I wonder?"

The course was empty.

"Tortoise got away with her!" laughed Wally.

"H'm," said Jim. "We'll track her to her lair."

In her lair — the kitchen — Mrs. Brown was discovered, modestly hiding behind the door. The tortoise was on the table, apparently cheerful.

"Poor dear pet!" said Mrs. Brown. "He wouldn't run. I don't think he was awake to the situation, Master Jim, dear, so I just carried him over — I didn't think it mattered which way I ran — and my scones were in the oven! They're just out — perhaps you'd all try them?" — this insinuatingly. "I don't think this tortoise comes of a racing family!" And the great menagerie race concluded happily in the kitchen in what Wally called "a hot buttered orgy."

CHAPTER 4

Jim's Idea

TWO hammocks, side by side, under a huge pine tree, swung lazily to and fro in the evening breeze. In them Norah and Harry rocked happily, too comfortable, as Norah said, to talk. They had all been out riding most of the day, and were happily tired. Tea had been discussed fully, and everything was exceedingly peaceful.

Footsteps at racing speed sounded far off on the gravel of the front path — a wide sweep that ran round the broad lawn. There was a scatter of stones, and then a thud-thud over the grass to the pine trees — sounds that signalled the arrival of Jim and Wally, in much haste. Jim's hurry was so excessive that he could not pull himself up in time to avoid Harry. He bumped violently into the hammock, with the natural result that Harry swung sharply against Norah, and for a moment things were rather mixed.

"You duffer!" growled Harry, steadying his rocking bed. "Hurt you?" — this to Norah.

"No thanks," Norah laughed. "What's the matter with you two?"

"Got an idea," Wally gasped, fanning himself with a pine cone.

"Hurt you?"

"Rather. It's always a shock for me to have an idea. Anyway this isn't mine — it's Jim's."

"Oh." Norah's tone was more respectful. Jim's ideas were not to be treated lightly as a rule. "Well, let's hear it."

"Fishing," Jim said laconically. "Let's start out at the very daybreak, and get up the river to Anglers' Bend. They say you can always get fish there. We'll ride, and take Billy to carry the tucker and look for bait. Spend the whole blessed day, and come home with the mopokes. What do you chaps say?"

"Grand idea!" Norah cried, giving her hammock an ecstatic swing. "We'll have to fly round, though. Did you ask Dad?"

"Yes, and he said we could go. It's tucker that's the trouble. I don't know if we're too late to arrange about any."

"Come and ask Mrs. Brown," said Norah, flinging a pair of long legs over the edge of the hammock. "She'll fix us up if she can."

They tore off to the kitchen and arrived panting. Mrs. Brown was sitting in calm state on the kitchen verandah, and greeted them with a wide, expansive smile. Norah explained their need.

Mrs. Brown pursed up her lips.

"I haven't anything fancy, my dear," she said slowly. "Only plum cake and scones, and there's a nice cold tongue, and an apple pie. I'd like you to have tarts, but the fire's out. Do you think you could manage?"

Jim laughed.

"I guess that'll do, Mrs. Brown," he said. "We'll live like fighting cocks, and bring you home any amount of fish for breakfast. Don't you worry about sandwiches, either — put in a loaf or two of bread, and a chunk of butter, and we'll be right as rain."

"Then I'll have it all packed for you first thing, Master Jim," Mrs. Brown declared.

"That's ripping," said the boys in a breath. "Come and find Billy."

Billy was dragged from the recesses of the stable. He grinned widely with joy at the prospect of the picnic.

"All the ponies ready at five, Billy," ordered Jim. "Yours too. We're going to make a day of it — and we'll want bait. Now, you chaps, come along and get lines and hooks ready!"

"Whirr-i-r!"

The alarm clock by Jim's bedside shrieked suddenly in the first hint of daylight, and Jim sprang from his pillow with the alertness of a Jack-in-the-box, and grabbed the clock, to stop its further eloquence. He sat down on the edge of his bed, and yawned tremendously. At the other side of the room Harry slept peacefully. Nearer Wally's black eyes twinkled for a moment, and hurriedly closed, apparently in deep slumber. He snored softly.

"Fraud!" said Jim, with emphasis. He seized his pillow, and hurled it vigorously. It caught Wally on the face and stayed there, and beneath its shelter the victim still snored on serenely.

Jim rose with deliberation and, seizing the bedclothes, gave a judicious pull, which ended in Wally's suddenly finding himself on the floor. He clasped wildly at the blankets, but they were dragged from his reluctant grasp. Jim's toe stirred him gently and at length he rose.

"Beast!" he said miserably. "What on earth's the good of getting up at this hour?"

"Got to make an early start," replied his host. "Come and stir up old Harry." Harry was noted as a sleeper. Pillows hurled on top of him were as nought. The bedclothes were removed, but he turned on his side and slumbered like a little child.

"And to think," Wally said, "that that chap springs up madly when the getting-up bell rings once at school!"

"School was never like this," Jim grinned. "There's the squirt, Wal."

The squirt was there; so was the jug of water, and a moment sufficed to charge the weapon. The nozzle was gently inserted into the sleeper's pyjama collar, and in a moment the drenched and wrathful hero arose majestically from his watery pillow and, seizing his tormentors, banged their heads together with great effect.

"You're slow to wake, but no end of a terror when once you rouse up," said Wally, ruefully rubbing his pate.

"Goats!" said Harry briefly, rubbing his neck with a hard towel. "Come on and have a swim."

They tore down the hall, only pausing at Norah's door while Jim ran in to wake her — a deed speedily accomplished by gently and firmly pressing a wet sponge upon her face. Then they raced to the lagoon, and in a few minutes were splashing and ducking in the water. They spent more time there than Jim had intended, their return being delayed by a spirited boat race between Harry's slippers, conducted by Wally and Jim. By the time Harry had rescued his sopping footgear, the offenders were beyond pursuit in the middle of the lagoon, so he contented himself with annexing Jim's slippers, in which he proudly returned to the house. Jim, arriving just too late to save his own, promptly "collared" those of Wally, leaving the last-named youth no alternative but to paddle home in the water-logged slippers — the ground being too rough and stony to admit of barefoot travelling.

Norah, fresh from the bath, was prancing about the verandah in her kimono as the boys raced up to the house, her hair a dusky cloud about her face.

"Not dressed? — you laziness!" Jim flung at her.

"Well, you aren't either," was the merry retort.

"No; but we've got no silly hair to brush!"

"Pooh! — that won't take me any time. Mrs. Brown's up, Jim, and she says breakfast will be ready in ten minutes."

"Good old Brownie!" Jim ejaculated. "Can't beat her, can you? D'you know if she's got the swag packed?"

"Everything's packed, and she's given it all to Billy, and it's on old Polly by now." Polly was the packhorse. "Such a jolly, big bundle — and everything covered over with cabbage leaves to keep it cool."

"Hooroo for Casey! Well, scurry and get dressed, old girl. I bet you keep us waiting at the last."

"I'm sure I won't," was the indignant answer, as Norah ran off through the hall. "Think of how much longer you take over your breakfast!"

Ten minutes later breakfast smoked on the wide kitchen table, Mrs. Brown, like a presiding goddess, flourishing a big spoon by a frying-pan that sent up a savoury odour.

"I'm sure I hope you'll all kindly excuse having it in here," she said in pained tones. "No use to think of those lazy hussies of girls having the breakfast-room ready at this hour. So I thought as how you wouldn't mind."

"Mind! — not much, Mrs. Brown," Jim laughed. "You're too good to us altogether. Eggs and bacon! Well, you are a brick! Cold tucker would have done splendidly for us."

"Cold, indeed! — not if I know it — and you precious lambs off for such a ride, and going to be hot weather and all," said the breathless Mrs. Brown indignantly. "Now, you just eat a good breakfast, Miss Norah, my love. I've doughnuts here, nearly done, nice and puffy and brown, just as you like them, so hurry up and don't let your bacon get cold."

There was not, indeed, much chance for the bacon which disappeared in a manner truly alarming, while its fate was speedily shared by the huge pile of crisp doughnuts which Mrs. Brown presently placed upon the table with a flourish.

"We don't get things like this at school!" Wally said regretfully, pausing for an instant before his seventh.

"All the more reason you should eat plenty now," said their constructor, holding the dough-nuts temptingly beneath his nose. "Come now, dearie, do eat something!" and Wally bashfully recommenced his efforts.

"How's Billy getting on?" Jim inquired.

"Billy's in the back kitchen, Master Jim, my love, and you've no call to worry your head about him. He's had three plates of bacon and five eggs, and most like by this time he's finished all his doughnuts and drunk his coffee-pot dry. That young man will eat anything," concluded Mrs. Brown solemnly.

"Well, I can't eat anything more, anyhow," Jim declared. "How we're all going to ride fifteen miles beats me. If we sleep all day, instead of catching fish for you, you've only got yourself to blame, Mrs. Brown." Whereat Mrs. Brown emitted fat and satisfied chuckles, and the meeting broke up noisily, and rushed off to find its hats.

Six ponies in a line against the stable yard fence — Bobs, with an eye looking round hopefully for Norah and sugar; Mick, most feather-headed of chestnuts, and Jim's especial delight; Topsy and Barcoo, good useful station ponies, with plenty of fun, yet warranted not to break the necks of boy-visitors; Bung Eye, a lean piebald, that no one but black Billy ever thought of riding; next to him old Polly, packed securely with the day's provisions. Two fishing-rods struck out from her bundles, and a big bunch of hobbles jingled as she moved.

There was nothing in the saddles to distinguish Norah's mount, for she, too, rode astride. Mr. Linton had a rooted dislike to side saddles, and was wont to say he preferred horses with sound withers and a daughter whose right hip was not higher than her left. So Norah rode on a dainty little hunting saddle like Jim's, her habit being a neat divided skirt, which had the double advantage of looking nice on horseback, and having no bothersome tail to hold up when off.

The boys were dressed without regard to appearances — loose old coats and trousers, soft shirts and leggings. Red-striped towels, peeping out of Polly's packs, indicated that Jim had not forgotten the possibilities of bathing which the creek afforded. A tin teapot jangled cheerfully against a well-used black billy.

"All right, you chaps?" Jim ran his eye over the ponies and their gear. "Better have a look at your girths. Come along."

Norah was already in the saddle, exulting over the fact that, in spite of Jim's prophecy that she would be late, she was the first to be mounted. Bobs was prancing happily, infected with the gaiety of the moment, the sweet morning air and sunshine, and the spirit of mirth that was everywhere. Mick joined him in capering, as Jim swung himself into the saddle. Billy, leading Polly, and betraying an evident distaste for a task which so hampered the freedom of his movements, moved off down the track.

Just as Wally and Harry mounted, a tall figure in pyjamas appeared at the gate of the back yard.

"There's Dad!" Norah cried gleefully, cantering up to him. The boys followed.

"Had to get up to see the last of you," Mr. Linton said. "Not much chance of sleeping anyhow, with you rowdy people about."

"Did we wake you, Dad? — sorry."

"Very sorry, aren't you?" Mr. Linton laughed at the merry face. "Well, take care of yourselves; remember, Norah's in your charge, Jim, and all the others in yours, Norah! Keep an eye to your ponies, and don't let them stray too far, even if they are hobbled. And mind you bring me home any amount of fish, Harry and Wal."

"We will, sir," chorused the boys.

Norah leant from her saddle and slipped an arm round her father's neck.

"Goodbye, Dad, dear."

"Goodbye, my little girl. Be careful — don't forget." Mr. Linton kissed her fondly. "Well, you're all in a hurry — and so am I, to get back to bed! So-long, all of you. Have a good time."

"So-long!" The echoes brought back the merry shout as the six ponies disappeared round the bend in the track.

Down the track to the first gate helter-skelter — Billy, holding it open, showed his white teeth in a broad grin as the merry band swept through. Then over the long grass of the broad paddock, swift hoofs shaking off the dewdrops that yet hung sparkling in the sunshine. Billy plodded far behind with the packhorse, envy in his heart and discontent with the fate that kept him so far in the rear, compelled to progress at the tamest of jogs.

The second paddock traversed, they passed through the sliprails into a bush paddock known as the Wide Plain. It was heavily timbered towards one end, where the river formed its boundary, but towards the end at which they entered was almost cleared, only a few logs lying here and there, and occasionally a tall dead tree.

"What a place for a gallop!" said Harry. His quiet face was flushed and his eyes sparkling.

"Look at old Harry!" jeered Wally. "He's quite excited. Does your mother know you're out, Hal?"

"I'll punch you, young Wally," retorted Harry. "Just you be civil. But isn't it a splendid place? Why, there's a clear run for a mile, I should say."

"More than that," Jim answered. "We've often raced here."

"Oh!" Norah's eyes fairly danced. "Let's have a race now!"

"Noble idea!" exclaimed Wally.

"Well, it'll have to be a handicap to make it fair," Jim said. "If we start level, Norah's pony can beat any of the others, and I think Mick can beat the other two. At any rate we'll give you fellows a start, and Norah must give me one."

"I don't care," Norah said gleefully, digging her heel into Bobs, with the result that that animal suddenly executed a bound in mid-air. "Steady, you duffer; I didn't mean any offence, Bobsie dear." She patted his neck.

"I should think you wouldn't care," Jim said. "Best pony and lightest weight! You ought to be able to leave any of us miles behind, so we'll give you a beautiful handicap, young woman!"

"Where's the winning post?" Harry asked.

"See that big black tree — the one just near the boundary fence, I mean? It's a few chains from the fence, really. We'll finish there," Jim replied.

"Come on, then," said Norah, impatiently. "Get on ahead, Harry and Wally; you'll have to sing out

'Go!' Jim, and sing it out loud, 'cause we'll be ever
so far apart."

"Right oh!" Jim said. "Harry, clear on a good
way; you're the heaviest. Pull up when I tell you;
you, too, Wal." He watched the two boys ride on
slowly, and sang out to them to stop when he
considered they had received a fair start. Then he
rode on himself until he was midway between
Wally and Norah, Harry some distance ahead of
the former. The ponies had an inkling of what was
in the wind, and were dancing with impatience.

"Now then, Norah," — Jim flung a laughing look
over his shoulder — "no cribbing there!"

"I'm not!" came an indignant voice.

"All right — don't! Ready, everyone? Then —
go!"

As the word "Go" left Jim's lips the four ponies
sprang forward sharply, and a moment later were
in full gallop over the soft springy turf. It was an
ideal place for a race — clear ground, covered with
short soft grass, well eaten off by the sheep — no
trees to bar the way, and over all a sky of the
brightest blue, flecked by tiny, fleecy cloudlets.

They tore over the paddock, shouting at the
ponies, laughing, hurling defiance at each other.
At first Harry kept his lead; but weight will tell,
and presently Wally was almost level with him,
with Jim not far behind. Bobs had not gone too
well at first — he was too excited to get thoroughly
into his stride, and had spent his time in dancing
when he should have been making up his
handicap.

When, however, he did condescend to gallop, the
distance that separated him from the other ponies

was rapidly overhauled. Norah, leaning forward in
her stirrups, her face alight with eagerness, urged
him on with voice and hand — she rarely, if ever,
touched him with a whip at any time. Quickly she
gained on the others; now Harry was caught and
passed, even as Jim caught Wally and deprived
him of the lead he had gaily held for some time.
Wally shouted laughing abuse at him, flogging his
pony on the while.

Now Norah was neck and neck with Wally, and
slowly she drew past him and set sail after Jim.
That she could beat him she knew very well, but
the question was, was there time to catch him?
The big tree which formed the winning post was
very near now. "Scoot, Bobsie, dear!" whispered
Norah, employing a piece of Jim's schoolboy slang.
At any rate, Bobs understood, for he went forward
with a bound. They were nearly level with Jim
now — Wally, desperately flogging, close in the
rear.

At that moment Jim's pony put his foot into a
hole, and went down like a shot rabbit, bowling
over and over. Jim, flung like a stone out of a
catapult, landed some distance ahead of the pony.
He, too, rolled for a moment, and then lay still.

It seemed to Norah that she pulled Bobs up
almost in his stride. Certainly she was off before
he had fairly slackened to a walk, throwing herself
wildly from the saddle. She tore up to Jim — Jim,
who lay so horribly still.

"Jim — dear Jim!" she cried. She took his head
on her knee. "Jim — oh, Jim, do speak to me!"

There was no sound. The boy lay motionless,

his tanned face strangely white. Harry, coming up, jumped off, and ran to his side.

"Is he hurt much?"

"I don't know — no, don't you say he's hurt much — he couldn't be, in such a second! Jim — dear — speak, old chap!" A big sob rose in her throat, and choked her at the heavy silence. Harry took Jim's wrist in his hand, and felt with fumbling fingers for the pulse. Wally, having pulled his pony up with difficulty, came tearing back to the little group.

"Is he killed?" he whispered, awestruck.

A little shiver ran through Jim's body. Slowly he opened his eyes, and stretched himself

"What's up?" he said weakly. "Oh, I know ... Mick?"

"He's all right, darling," Norah said, with a quivering voice. "Are you hurt much?"

"Bit of a bump on my head," Jim said, struggling to a sitting position. He rubbed his forehead. "What's up, Norah?" For the brown head had gone down on his knee and the shoulders were shaking.

Jim patted her head very gently.

"You dear old duffer," he said tenderly.

CHAPTER 5

Anglers' Bend

JIM's "bump on the head" luckily proved not very serious. A handkerchief, soaked in the creek by Wally, who rode there and back at a wild gallop, proved an effective bandage applied energetically by Harry, who had studied "first-aid" in an ambulance class. Ten minutes of this treatment, however, proved as much as Jim's patience would stand, and at the end of that time he firmly removed the handkerchief, and professed himself cured.

"Nothing to make a fuss about, anyhow," he declared, in answer to sympathetic inquiries. "Head's a bit 'off,' but nothing to grumble at. It'll be all right, if we ride along steadily for a while. I don't think I'll do any more racing just now though, thank you!"

"Who won that race?" queried Harry, laughing. The spirits of the little party, from being suddenly at zero, had gone up with a bound.

"Blessed if I know," said Jim. "I only know I was leading until Mick ended matters for me."

"I led after that, anyhow," said Wally. "Couldn't pull my beauty up, he was so excited by Mick's somersault."

"I'd have won, in the long run!" Norah said.

There were still traces of tears in her eyes, but
her face was merry enough. She was riding very
close to Jim.

"Yes, I think you would," Jim answered. "You
and Bobs were coming up like a hurricane last
time I looked round. Never mind, we'll call it
anybody's race and have it over again sometime."

They rode along for a few miles, keeping close
to the river, which wound in and out, fringed with
a thick belt of scrub, amongst which rose tall
red-gum trees. Flights of cockatoos screamed over
their heads, and magpies gurgled in the thick
shades by the water. Occasionally came the clear
whistle of a lyre bird or the peal of a laughing
jackass. Jim knew all the bird-notes, as well as
the signs of bush game, and pointed them out as
they rode. Once a big wallaby showed for an
instant, and there was a general outcry and a
plunge in pursuit, but the wallaby was too quick
for them, and found a safe hiding-place in the
thickest of the scrub, where the ponies could not
follow.

"We cross the creek up here," Jim said, "and
make 'cross country a bit. It saves several miles."

"How do you cross? Bridge?" queried Wally.

"Bridge! — don't grow such things in this part
of the world," laughed Jim. "No, there's a place
where it's easy enough to ford, a little way up.
There are plenty of places fordable, if you only
know them, on this creek; but a number of them
are dangerous, because of deep holes and boggy
places. Father lost a good horse in one of those
bogs, and to look at the place you'd only have
thought it a nice level bit of grassy ground."

"My word?" Wally whistled. "What a bit of hard luck!"

"Yes, it was, rather," Jim said. "It made us careful about crossing, I can tell you. Even the men look out since Harry Wilson got bogged another time, trying to get over after a bullock. Of course he wouldn't wait to go round, and he had an awful job to get his horse out of the mud — it's something like a quicksand. After that father had two or three good crossings made very plain and clear, and whenever a new man is put on they're explained to him. See, there's one now."

They came suddenly on a gap in the scrub, leading directly to the creek, which was, indeed, more of a river than a creek, and in winter ran in a broad, rapid stream. Even in summer it ran always, though the full current dwindled to a trickling, sluggish streamlet, with here and there a deep, quiet pool, where the fish lay hidden through the long hot days.

All the brushwood and trees had been cleared away, leaving a broad pathway to the creek. At the edge of the gap a big board, nailed to a tall tree, bore the word FORD in large letters. Farther on, between the trees, a glimpse of shining water caught the eye.

"That's the way father's had all the fords marked," Norah said. "He says it's no good running risks for the sake of a little trouble."

"Dad's always preaching that," Jim observed. "He says people are too fond of putting up with makeshifts, that cost ever so much more time and trouble than it does to do a thing thoroughly at the start. So he always makes us do a thing just

as well as we know how, and there's no end of
rows if he finds anyone 'half doing' a job. 'Begin
well and finish better,' he says. My word, it gives
you a lesson to see how he fixes a thing himself."

"Dear old Dad," said Norah softly, half to
herself.

"I think your father's just splendid," Harry said
enthusiastically. "He does give you a good time,
too."

"Yes, I know he does," Jim said. "I reckon he's
the best man that ever lived! All the same, he
doesn't mean to give me a good time always. When
I leave school I've got to work and make my own
living, with just a start from him. He says he's
not going to bring any boy up to be a loafer." Jim's
eyes grew soft. "I mean to show him I can work,
too," he said.

They were at the water's edge, and the ponies
gratefully put their heads down for a drink of the
cool stream that clattered and danced over its
stony bed. After they had finished, Jim led the
way through the water, which was only deep
enough to wash the ponies' knees. When they had
climbed the opposite bank, a wide, grassy plain
stretched before them.

"We cut across here," Norah explained, "and
pick up the creek over there — that saves a good
deal."

"Does Billy know this cut?" Harry queried.

"What doesn't Billy know?" Norah laughed.
"Come along."

They cantered slowly over the grass. remembering that Jim was scarcely fit yet for violent
exercise, though he stoutly averred that his

accident had left no traces whatever. The sun was getting high and it *was* hot, away from the cool shade near the creek. Twice a hare bounded off in the grass, and once Harry jumped off hurriedly and killed a big brown snake that was lazily sunning itself upon a broad log.

"I do hate those beasts!" he said, remounting. Norah had held his pony for him.

"So do I," she nodded, "only one gets used to them. Father found one on his pillow the other night."

"By George!" Harry said. "Did he kill it?"

"Well, rather. They are pretty thick here, especially a bit earlier than this. One got into the kitchen through the window, by the big vine that grows outside, and when Mrs. Brown pulled down the blind it came, too — it was on the roller. That was last Christmas, and Mrs. Brown says she's shaking still!"

"Snakes are rummy things," Harry observed. "Ever hear that you can charm them with music?"

"I've heard it," Norah said quaintly. Her tone implied that it was a piece of evidence she did not accept on hearsay.

"Well, I believe it's true. Last summer a whole lot of us were out on the verandah, and there was plenty of laughing and talking going on — a snake wouldn't crawl into a rowdy group like that for the fun of it, now, would he? It was Christmas day, and my little brother Phil — he's six — had found a piccolo in his stocking, and he was sitting on the end of the verandah playing away at this thing. We thought it was a bit of a row, but Phil was quite happy. Presently my sister Vera looked at him, and screamed out, 'Why, there's a snake!'

"So there was, and it was just beside Phil. It had crawled up between the verandah boards, and was lying quietly near the little chap, looking at him stealthily — he was blowing away, quite unconcerned. We didn't know what to do for a moment, for the beastly thing was so near Phil that we didn't like to hit it for fear we missed and it bit him. However, Phil solved the difficulty by getting up and walking off, still playing the piccolo. The snake never stirred when he did — and you may be sure it didn't get much chance to stir after. Three sticks came down on it at the same time."

"I say!" Norah breathed quickly. "What an escape for poor Phil!"

"Wasn't it?" He didn't seem to care a bit when we showed him the snake and told him it had been so near him — he hadn't known a thing about it. 'Can't be bovvered wiv snakes,' was all he said."

"When I was a little kiddie," Norah said, "they found me playing with a snake one day."

"Playing with it?" Harry echoed.

"Yes; I was only about two, and I don't remember anything about it. Dad came on to the back verandah, and saw me sitting by a patch of dust, stroking something. He couldn't make out what it was at first, and then he came a bit nearer, and saw that it was a big snake. It was lying in the dust sunning itself, and I was stroking it most kindly."

"By George!" said Harry.

"Funny what things kiddies will do!" said

Norah, with all the superiority of twelve long
years. "It frightened Dad tremendously. He didn't
know what to do, 'cause he didn't dare come near
or call out. I s'pose the snake saw him, 'cause it
began to move. It crawled right over my bare legs."

"And never bit you?"

"No; I kept on stroking its back as it went over
my knees, without the least idea that it was
anything dangerous. Dad said it seemed years and
years before it went right over and crawled away
from me into the grass. He had me out of the way
in about half a second, and got a stick, and I cried
like anything when he killed it and said he was
naughty!"

"If you chaps have finished swapping snake
yarns," said Jim, turning in his saddle, "there's
Anglers' Bend."

They had been riding steadily across the plain,
until they had again come near the scrub-line
which marked the course of the creek. Following
the direction pointed by Jim's finger, they saw a
deep curve in the green, where the creek suddenly
left the fairly straight course it had been pursuing
and made two great bends something like a capital
U, the points of which lay in their direction. They
rode down between them until they were almost
at the water's edge.

Here the creek was very deep, and in sweeping
round had cut out a wide bed, nearly three times
its usual breadth. Tall trees grew almost to the
verge of the banks on both sides, so that the water
was almost always in shadow, while so high were
the banks that few breezes were able to ripple its
surface. It lay placid all the year, scarcely troubled

even in winter, when the other parts of the creek rushed and tumbled in flood. There was room in the high banks of Anglers' Bend for all the extra water, and its presence was only marked by the strength of the current that ran in the very centre of the stream.

Just now the water was not high, and seemed very far below the children, who sat looking at it from their ponies on the bank. As they watched in silence a fish leaped in the middle of the Bend. The sudden movement seemed amazing in the stillness. It flashed for an instant in a patch of sunlight, and then fell back, sending circling ripples spreading to each bank.

"Good omen, I hope," Harry said, "though they often don't bite when they jump, you know."

"It's not often they don't bite here," Jim said.

"Well, it looks a good enough place for anything — if we can't catch fish here, we won't be up to much as anglers," Harry said.

"You've been here before, haven't you, Norah?" Wally asked.

"Oh, yes; ever so many times."

"Father and Norah have great fishing excursions on their own," said Jim. "They take a tent and camp out for two or three days with Billy as general helper. I don't know how many whales they haven't caught at this place. They know the Bend as well as anyone."

"Well, I guess we'd better take off the saddles and get to work," said Norah, slipping off Bobs and patting his neck before undoing the girth. The boys followed her example and soon the saddles

were safely stowed in the shade. Then Jim turned
with a laugh.

"Well, we *are* duffers," he said. "Can't do a thing
till Billy turns up. He's got all the hooks and lines,
all the bait, all the hobbles, all the everything!"

"Whew-w!" whistled the boys.

"Well, it doesn't matter," Norah said cheerfully.
"There's lots to do. We can hang up the ponies
while we hunt for rods. You boys have got your
strong knives, haven't you?"

They had, and immediately scattered to work.
The ponies having been tied securely under a
grove of saplings, the search for rods began, and
soon four long straight sticks were obtained with
the necessary amount of "springiness." Then they
hunted for a suitable camping-ground, where
lunch might be eaten without too much disturb-
ance from flies and mosquitoes, and gathered a
good supply of dry sticks for a fire.

"Billy ought to bless us, anyhow," Jim grinned.

"Yes, oughtn't he? Come along and see if he's
coming." They ran out upon the plain, and cheerful
exclamations immediately proclaimed the fact that
Billy and the old packhorse had at length made
their appearance in what Wally called the "offing."

Billy soon clattered up to the little party, the
hobbles and quart pot jingling cheerfully on old
Polly's back. He grinned amiably at the four merry
faces awaiting him in the shade of a wattle tree.

"This feller pretty slow," he said, indicating
Polly with a jerk of his thumb. "You all waitin' for
tackle?"

"Rather," said Jim. "Never mind, we've got
everything ready. Look sharp and shy down the

hooks, Billy — they're in that tin, and the lines are tied on to it, in a parcel. That's right," as the black boy tossed the tackle down and he caught it deftly. "Now, you chaps, get to work, and get your lines ready."

"Right oh!" said the chorus, as it fell to work. Billy made a swift incursion into the interior of the pack, and fished up a tin of worms and some raw meat, Wally being the only one to patronise the latter. The other three baited their hooks with worms, and, all being in readiness, made their way down the steep bank at a place where a little cleft gave easier access to a tiny shelving beach below. Here a great tree-trunk had long ago been left by an unusually high flood, and formed a splendid place to fish from, as it jutted out for some distance over the stream. Norah scrambled out like a cat to its farthest extremity, and Harry followed her for part of the way. Wally and Jim settled themselves at intervals along the trunk. Sinkers, floats and baits were examined, and the business of the day began.

Everybody knows how it feels to fish. You throw in your hook with such blissful certainty that no fish can possibly resist the temptation you are dangling before its eyes. There is suppressed excitement all over you. You are all on the alert, feeling for imaginary nibbles, for bites that are not there. Sometimes, of course, the dreams come true, and the bites are realities; but these occasions are sadly outnumbered by the times when you keep on feeling and bobbing your line vainly, while excitement lulls to expectation, and expectation merges into hope, and hope becomes wishing, and wishing often dies down to disappointment.

Such was the gradual fate of the fishing party at Anglers' Bend. At first the four floats were watched with an intensity of regard that should surely have had some effect in luring fishes to the surface; but as the minutes dragged by and not a fish seemed inclined even to nibble, the solemn silence which had brooded on the quartet was broken by sundry fidgetings and wrigglings and suppressed remarks on the variableness of fish and the slowness of fishing. Men enjoy the sport, because they can light their pipes and smoke in expectant ease; but the consolation of tobacco was debarred from boys who were, as Jim put it, "too young to smoke and too old to make idiots of themselves by trying it," and so they found it undeniably dull.

Billy came down to join the party presently, after he had seen to his horses and unpacked old Polly's load. His appearance gave Jim a brilliant idea, and he promptly despatched the black boy for cake, which proved a welcome stimulant to flagging enthusiasm.

"Don't know if fish care about cake crumbs," said Harry, finishing a huge slice with some regret.

"Didn't get a chance of sampling any of mine," Wally laughed. "I wanted it all myself. Hallo!"

"What is it — a bite?"

"Rather — such a whopper! I've got it, too," Wally gasped, tugging at his line.

"You've got it, right enough," Jim said. "Why, your rod's bending right over. Want a hand?"

"No, thanks — manage it myself," said the fisherman, tugging manfully. "Here she comes!"

The line came in faster now, and the strain on the rod was plain. Excitement ran high.

"It's a great big perch, I do believe," Norah exclaimed. "Just fancy, if it beats Dad's big boomer — the biggest ever caught here."

"It'll beat some records," Wally gasped, hauling in frantically. "Here she comes!"

"She" came, with a final jerk. Jim broke into a suppressed shout of laughter. For Wally's catch was nothing less than an ancient, mud-laden boot!

CHAPTER 6

A Bush Fire

WALLY disentangled his hook gravely, while
the others would have laughed more heartily
but for fear of frightening the fish.

"Well, I'm blessed!" said the captor at length,
surveying the prize with his nose in the air. "A
blooming old boot! Been there since the year one,
I should think, by the look of it."

"I thought you had a whale at the very least,"
grinned Harry.

"Well, I've broken my duck, anyhow, and that's
more than any of you others can say!" Wally
laughed. "Time enough for you to grin when you've
caught something yourselves — even if it's only
an old boot! It's a real old stager and no mistake.
I wonder how it came in here."

"Some poor old beggar of a swaggie, I expect,"
Jim said. "He didn't chuck it away until it was
pretty well done, did he? Look at the holes in the
uppers — and there's no sole left to speak of."

"Do you see many tramps here?" Harry asked.

"Not many — we're too far from a road," Jim
replied. "Of course there are a certain number who
know of the station, and are sure of getting tucker
there — and a job if they want one — not that
many of them do, the lazy beggars. Most of them

would be injured if you asked them to chop a bit
of wood in return for a meal, and some of them
threaten to set the place on fire if they don't get
all they want."

"My word!" said Wally. "Did they ever do it?"

"Once — two years ago," Jim answered. "A
fellow came one hot evening in January. We'd had
a long spell of heat, and all our meat had gone
bad that day; there was hardly a bit in the place,
and of course they couldn't kill a beast till evening.
About the middle of the day this chap turned up
and asked for tucker.

"Mrs. Brown gave him bread and flour and tea
and some cake — a real good haul for any swaggie.
It was too good for this fellow, for he immediately
turned up his proud nose and said he wanted
meat. Mrs. Brown explained that she hadn't any
to give him; but he evidently didn't believe her,
said it was our darned meanness and, seeing no
men about, got pretty insulting. At last he tried
to force his way past Mrs. Brown into the kitchen."

"Did he get in?" asked Wally.

"Nearly — not quite, though. Dad and Norah
and I had been out riding, and we came home,
past the back yard, in the nick of time. We couldn't
hear what the fellow was saying to Mrs. Brown,
but his attitude was enough to make us pull up,
and as we did so we saw him try to shove her
aside. She was plucky enough and banged the door
in his face, but he got his foot in the crack, so that
it couldn't shut, and began to push it open.

"Dad slipped off his horse gently. He made a
sign to us to keep quiet and went across the yard,
and we saw him shake the lash of his stockwhip

loose. You can just fancy how Norah and I were dancing with joy!

"Dad was just near the verandah when we saw the door give. Poor old Brownie was getting the worst of it. We heard the fellow call out something — a threat — and Dad's arm went up, and the stockwhip came down like a flash across the man's shoulder. He gave one yell! You never heard such an amazed and terrified roar in your life!" and Jim chuckled with joy at the recollection.

"He turned on Dad and jumped at him, but he got another one with the whip that made him pause, and then Dad caught him and shook him like a rat. Mr. Swaggie was limp enough when it was over.

" 'I've a very good mind to give you in charge!' Dad said — he was simply furious. It made a fellow feel pretty bad to see poor old Brownie's white face in the doorway, and to think what a fright she had had.

"The swaggie turned a very ugly look on Dad.

" 'You give me in charge, and I'll precious quick have you up for assault!' he said.

"Dad laughed.

" 'As for that, you can do exactly as you choose,' he said. 'I'll be quite ready to answer for thrashing a cur like you. However, you're not worth carting seventeen miles to Cunjee, so you can go — the quicker the better.' "

"And he cleared, I suppose?" Wally asked.

"He just did — went like a redshank. But when he got outside the gate and a bit away he stopped, and turned round and let fly at Dad — such a volley of threats and abuse you never heard. It

finished up with something about the grass; we
didn't quite understand what; but we remembered
it later, and then it was clearer to us. However,
he didn't stop to explain, as Dad turned the dogs
loose. They lost no time, and neither did the
swaggie. He left the place at about the rate of a
mile a minute!"

Jim paused.

"Thought I had a bite," he said, pulling up his
line. "Bother it! that bait's gone! Chuck me a
worm, young Wally." He impaled the worm and
flung his line out again.

"Where was I? Oh, yes. Norah and I were a bit
scared about the swaggie and wondered what he'd
try to do; but Dad only laughed at us. It never
entered his head that the brute would really try
to have his revenge. Of course it would have been
easy enough to have had him watched off the
place, but Dad didn't even think of it. He knows
better now.

"I waked up early next morning hearing some
one yelling outside. It was only just light. I slipped
out of my window and ran into the yard, and the
first thing I saw was smoke. It was coming from
the west, a great cloud of it, with plenty of wind
to help it along. It was one of those hot autumn
mornings — you know the kind. Make you feel
anyhow."

"Who was yelling?" asked Harry.

"One of Morrison's men — he owns the land
adjoining ours. This fellow was coo-eeing for all he
was worth.

" 'You'd better rouse your men out quick 'n'
lively,' he sang out. 'There's a big grass fire

between us and you. All our chaps are workin' at it; but I don't fancy they can keep it back in this wind.'

"I just turned and ran.

"The big bell we use for summoning the men to their meals hangs under the kitchen verandah and I made a beeline for it. There seemed plenty of rocks and bits of glass about, and my bare feet got 'em all — at least I thought so, — but there wasn't time to think much. Morrison's chap had galloped off as soon as he gave his news. I caught hold of the bell-pull and worked it all I knew!

"You should have seen them tumble out! In about half a minute the place was like a jumpers' nest that you've stirred up with a stick. Dad came out of the back door in his pyjamas, Norah came scudding along the verandah, putting on her kimono as she ran. Brownie and the other servants appeared at their windows, and the men came tumbling out of the barracks and the hut like so many rabbits.

"Dad was annoyed.

" 'What are you doing, you young donkey?' he rang out.

" 'Look over there!' I says, tugging the bell.

"Dad looked. It didn't take him long to see what was up when he spied that big cloud of smoke.

" 'Great Scott!' he shouted. 'Jim, get Billy to run the horses up. Where are you all? Burrows, Field, Henry! get out the water-cart — quick. All of you get ready fire-beaters. Dress yourselves — quickly!' (You could see that was quite an after-thought on Dad's part.) Then he turned and fled inside to dress."

"How ripping!" Wally said, wriggling on the log with joy.

"Ripping, do you call it?" said Jim indignantly. "You try it for yourself, young Wally, and see. Fire's not much of a joke when you're fighting it yourself, I can tell you. Well, Dad was out again in about two shakes, ready for the fray, and you can bet the rest of us didn't linger long. Billy had the horses up almost as soon, and everyone got his own. Things were a big merry in the stockyard, I can tell you, and heels did fly.

"After all, Norah here was the first mounted. Bobs was in the stable, you see, and Norah had him saddled before any of us had put our bridles on. Goodness knows how she dressed. I guess it wasn't much of a toilet!"

Jim ducked suddenly, and a chip hurled by Norah flew over his head and splashed into the water.

"Get out — you'll frighten the fish!" he said, grinning. "My yarn, old girl."

"Might have had the sense to keep me out of it," said Norah impolitely.

"You be jiggered," said Jim affectionately. "Anyhow, boys, you should have seen Dad's face when Norah trotted over from the stable. He was just girthing up old Bosun, and I was wrestling with Sirdar, who didn't want his crupper on.

" 'My dear child,' Dad said, 'get off that pony and go back to bed. You can't think I could allow you to come out?'

"Poor old Norah's face fell about a foot. She begged and argued, but she might as well have spared herself the trouble. At last Dad said she could ride out in the first two paddocks, but no nearer the fire, and she had to be content with that. I think she was pretty near mopping her eyes."

"Wasn't," said Norah indistinctly.

"Well, we went off. All of us had fire-beaters. You know we always have them ready; and Field was driving the water-cart — it always stands ready filled for use. We just galloped like mad. Dad didn't wait for any gates — Bosun can jump anything — and he just went straight across country. Luckily, there was no stock in the paddocks near the house, except that in one small paddock were about twenty valuable prize sheep. However, the fire was so far off that we reckoned they were safe, and so we turned our attention to the fire.

"We left old Norah in the second paddock, looking as miserable as a bandicoot. Dad made her promise not to meddle with the fire. 'Promise me you won't try any putting out on your own account,' he said; and Norah promised very reluctantly. I was jolly sorry you were out of it, you know, old kid," said Jim reflectively; and Norah gave him a little smile.

"We made great time across the paddocks," Jim continued. "Dad was ever so far ahead, of course, but our contingent, that had to go round by the gates, didn't do so badly. Billy was on Mick, and he and I had a go for the lead across the last paddock."

"Who won?" asked Harry.

"Me," said Jim ungrammatically. "When we got into the smoke we had to go round a bit, or we'd have gone straight into the fire. We hung up the horses in a corner that had been burnt round, and was safe from more fire, and off we went. There were ever so many men fighting it; all Morrison's fellows, and a lot from other places as well. The fire had started right at our boundary, and had come across a two-hundred acre paddock like a shot. Then a little creek checked it a bit, and let the fighters have a show.

"There were big trees blazing everywhere, and stumps and logs, and every few minutes the fire would get going again in some ferns or long grass, and go like mischief, and half a dozen men after it, to stop it. It had got across the creek, and there was a line of men on the bank keeping it back. Some others were chopping down the big, blazing, dead trees, that were simply showering sparks all round. The wind was pretty strong, and took burning leaves and sticks ever so far and started the fire in different places. Three fellows on ponies were doing nothing but watch for these flying firebrands, galloping after them and putting them out as they fell."

Jim paused.

"Say you put your hook in the water, Wally, old chap," he suggested.

Wally looked and blushed. In the excitement of the moment he had unconsciously pulled up his line until the bait dangled helplessly in the air, a foot above the water. The party on the log laughed at the expense of Wally, and Jim proceeded.

"Father and four other men came across the creek and sang to us —

" 'We're going back a bit to burn a break!' they said. 'Come along.'

"We all went back about a hundred yards from the creek and lit the grass, spreading out in a long line across the paddock. Then everyone kept his own little fire from going in the wrong direction, and kept it burning back towards the creek, of course preventing any logs or trees from getting alight. It was pretty tough work, the smoke was so bad, but at last it was done, and a big, burnt streak put across the paddock. Except for flying bits of lighted stuff there wasn't much risk of the fire getting away from us when once we had got that break to help us. You see, a grass fire isn't like a real bush fire. It's a far more manageable beast. It's when you get fire in thick scrub that you can just make up your mind to stand aside and let her rip!"

Jim pulled up his hook and examined his bait carefully.

"Fish seem off us," he said.

"That all the yarn?" Harry asked.

"No, there's more, if you're not sick of it."

"Well, fire away," Wally said impatiently. Jim let his sinker go down gently until it settled in comfort in the soft mud at the bottom.

"This is where I come to Norah," he said.

That young lady turned a lively red.

"If you're going to tell all that bosh about me, I'm off," she said, disgustedly. "Goodbye. You can call me when you've finished."

"Where are you off to, Norah?" inquired Harry.

"Somewhere to fish — I'm tired of you old gossips." Norah elevated a naturally tilted nose as she wound up her tackle and rose to her feet. She made her way along the log past the three boys until she reached the land, and, scrambling up the bank, vanished in the scrub. Presently they saw her reappear at a point a little lower down, where she ensconced herself in the roots of a tree that was sticking out of the bank, and looked extremely unsafe. She flung her line in below her perch.

"Hope she's all right," Harry said uneasily.

"You bet. Norah knows what she's about," Jim said calmly. "She can swim like a fish anyhow!"

"Well, go on with your yarn," urged Wally.

"Well — I told you how we stopped the fire at the little creek, didn't I? We thought it was pretty safe after we had burnt such a good break, and the men with axes had chopped down nearly all the big trees that were alight, so that they couldn't spread the fire. We reckoned we could sit down and mop our grimy brows and think what fine, brave, bold heroes we were! Which we did.

"There was one big tree the men couldn't get down. It was right on a bit of a hill, near the bank of the creek — a big brute of a tree, hollow for about twelve feet, and I don't know how high, but I'll bet it was over a hundred and fifty feet. It got alight from top to bottom, and, my word, didn't it blaze!

"The men tried to chop it down, but it was too hot a job even for a salamander. We could only watch it, and it took a lot of watching, because it was showering sparks and bits of wood, and blazing limbs and twigs in every direction. Lots of times they blew into the dead grass beyond our break, and it meant galloping to put them out.

"The wind had been pretty high all the time, and it got up suddenly to a regular gale. It caught this old tree and fairly whisked its burning limbs off. They flew ever so far. We thought we had them all out, when suddenly Dad gave a yell.

"There was a little, deep gully running at right angles to the creek, and right through the paddocks up to the house. In winter it was a creek, but now it was dry as a bone, and rank with dead grass at the bottom. As we looked we saw smoke rise from this gully, far away, in the home paddock.

"My Shropshires!" said Dad, and he made a run for Bosun.

"How we did tear! I never thought old Dad could run so hard! It seemed miles to the corner where the horses were, and ages before we got on them and were racing for the home paddock. And all the time the smoke was creeping along that beastly gully, and we knew well enough that, tear as we might, we couldn't be in time.

"You see, the valuable sheep were in a paddock where this gully ended. I wasn't very near the house, and no one might see the fire before every sheep was roasted. We had only just got them. Dad had imported some from England and some from Tasmania, and I don't know how much they hadn't cost."

"Weren't you afraid for the house as well?" asked Harry.

"No. There was a big ploughed paddock near the house; it would have taken a tremendous fire to get over that and the orchard and garden. We only worried about the Shropshires.

"I got the lead away, but Dad caught me up pretty soon. Between us and the sheep paddock there were only wire fences, which he wouldn't take Bosun over, so he couldn't race away from the rest of us this time.

" 'We might as well take it easy,' he said, 'for all the good we can do. The sheep nearly live in that gully.'

"All the same, we raced. The wind had gone down by now, so the fire couldn't travel as fast as it had done in the open ground. There was a long slope leading down to the gully, and as we got to this we could see the whole of the little paddock, and there wasn't a sheep in sight. Every blessed one was in the gully, and the fire was three-parts of the way along it!

" 'Roast mutton!' I heard Dad say under his breath.

"Then we saw Norah. She came racing on Bobs to the fence of the paddock near the head of the gully — much nearer the fire than we were. We saw her look at the fire and into the gully, and I reckon we all knew she was fighting with her promise to Dad about not tackling the fire. But she saw the sheep before we could. They had run from the smoke along the gully till they came to the head of it, where it ended with pretty steep banks all round. By that time they were thoroughly dazed, and there they would have stayed until they were roasted. Sheep are stupid brutes at any time, but in smoke they're just idiots!

"Norah gave only one look. Then she slipped off

Bobs and left him to look after himself, and she
tore down into the gully!"

"Oh, Jim, go on!" said Wally.

"I'm going," said Jim affably. "Dad gave one
shout as Norah disappeared into the gully. 'Go
back, my darling!' he yelled, forgetting that he was
so far off that he might as well have shouted to
the moon. Then he gave a groan, and dug his spurs
into Bosun. I had mine as far as they'd go in
Sirdar already!

"The smoke rolled on up the gully and in a
minute it had covered it all up. I thought it was
all up with Norah, too, and old Burrows behind
me was sobbing for all he was worth. We raced
and tore and yelled!

"Then we saw a sheep coming up out of the
smoke at the end of the gully. Another followed,
and another, and then more, until every blessed
one of the twenty was there (though we didn't stop
to count 'em then, I can tell you!). Last of all —
it just seemed years — came Norah!

"We could hear her shouting at the sheep before
we saw her. They were terribly hard to move. She
banged them with sticks, and the last old ram she
fairly kicked up the hill. They were just out of the
gully when the fire roared up it, and a minute or
so after that we got to her.

"Poor little kid; she was just black, and nearly
blind with the smoke. It was making her cry like
fun," said Jim, quite unconscious of his inap-
propriate smile. "I don't know if it was smoke in
his case, but so was Dad. We put the fire out quick
enough; it was easy work to keep it in the gully.
Indeed, Dad never looked at the fire, or the sheep

either. He just jumped off Bosun, and picked Norah up and held her as if she was a baby, and she hugged and hugged him. They're awfully fond of each other, Dad and Norah."

"And were the sheep all right?" Harry asked.

"Right as rain; not one of the black-faced beauties singed. It was a pretty close thing, you know," Jim said reminiscently. "The fire was just up to Norah as she got the last sheep up the hill; there was a hole burnt in the leg of her riding skirt. She told me afterwards she made up her mind she was going to die down in that beastly hole."

"My word, you must have been jolly proud of her!" Wally exclaimed. "Such a kid, too!"

"I guess we were pretty proud," Jim said quietly. "All the people about made no end of a fuss about her, and lots of kids would have been conceited over it all, but Norah never seemed to think a pennyworth about it. Fact is, her only thought at first was that Dad would think she had broken her promise to him. She looked up to him in the first few minutes, with her poor, swollen old eyes. 'I didn't forgot my promise, Dad, dear,' she said. 'I never touched the fire — only chased your silly old sheep!' "

"Was that the end of the fire?" Harry asked.

"Well, nearly. Of course we had to watch the burning logs and stumps for a few days, until all danger of more fires was over, and if there'd been a high wind in that time we might have had trouble. Luckily there wasn't any wind at all, and three days after there came a heavy fall of rain, which made everything safe. We lost about two hundred and fifty acres of grass, but in no time the paddock was green again, and the fire only did it good in the long run. We reckoned ourselves uncommonly lucky over the whole thing, though if Norah hadn't saved the Shropshires we'd have had to sing a different tune. Dad said he'd never shut up so much money in one small paddock again!"

Jim bobbed his float up and down despairingly. "This is the most fish-less creek!" he said. "Well, the only thing left to tell you is where the swagman came in."

"Oh, by Jove," Harry said, "I forgot the swaggie."

"Was it his fault the fire started?" inquired Wally.

"Rather! He camped under a bridge on the road that forms our boundary the night Dad cleared him off the place, and the next morning, very early, he deliberately lit our grass in three places, and then made off. He'd have got away, too, and nobody would have known anything about it, if it hadn't been for Len Morrison. You chaps haven't met Len, have you? He's a jolly nice fellow, older than me. I guess he's about sixteen now — perhaps seventeen.

"Len had a favourite cow, a great pet of his. He'd petted her as a calf and she'd follow him about like a dog. This cow was sick — they found her down in the paddock and couldn't move her, so they doctored her where she was. Len was awfully worried about her, and used to go to her late at night and first thing in the morning.

"He went out to the cow on this particular

morning about daylight. She was dead and so he
didn't stay; and he was riding back when he saw
the swagman lighting our grass. It was most
deliberately done. Len didn't go after him then.
He galloped up to his own place and gave the
alarm, and then he and one of their chaps cleared
out after the brute."

"Did they catch him?" Wally's eyes were dancing, and his sinker waved unconsciously in the air.

"They couldn't see a sign of him," Jim said. "The
road was a plain, straight one — you chaps know
it — the one we drove home on from the train. No
cover anywhere that would hide so much as a goat
— not even you, Wal! They followed it up for a
couple of miles, and then saw that he must have
gone across country somewhere. There was mighty
little cover there, either. The only possible hiding-
place was along the creek.

"He was pretty cunning — my word, he was!
He'd started up the road — Len had seen him —
and then he cut over the paddock at an angle,
back to the creek. That was why they couldn't find
any tracks when they started up the creek from
the road, and they made sure he had given them
the slip altogether.

"Len and the other fellow, a chap called Sam
Baker, pegged away up the creek as hard as they
could go, but feeling pretty blue about catching
the swaggie. Len was particularly wild, because
he'd made so certain he could lay his hands on
the fellow, and if he hadn't been sure, of course
he'd have stayed to help at the fire, and he didn't
like being done out of everything! They couldn't
understand not finding any tracks.

" 'Of course it's possible he's walked in the water,' Baker said.

" 'We'd have caught him by now if he had,' Len said. 'He couldn't get along quickly in the water. Anyhow, if I don't see anything of him before we get to the next bend, I'm going back to the fire.'

"They were nearly up to the bend, and Len was feeling desperate, when he saw a boot-mark half-way down the bank on the other side. He was over like a shot — the creek was very shallow — and there were tracks as plain as possible, leading down to the water!

"You can bet they went on then!

"They caught him a bit farther up. He heard them coming, and left his swag, so's he could get on quicker. They caught that first, and then they caught him. He had 'planted' in a clump of scrub, and they nearly passed him, but Len caught sight of him, and they had him in a minute."

"Did he come easily?" asked Wally.

"Rather not! He sent old Len flying — gave him an awful black eye. Len was up again at him like a shot, and I reckon it was jolly plucky of a chap of Len's age, and I dare say he'd have had an awful hiding if Sam hadn't arrived on the scene. Sam is a big, silent chap, and he can fight anybody in this district. He landed the swaggie first with one fist and then with the other, and the swaggie reckoned he'd been struck by a thunderbolt when they fished him out of the creek, where he had rolled! You see, Sam's very fond of Len, and it annoyed him to see his eye.

"The swaggie did not do any more resisting. He was like a half-dead, drowned rat. Len and Sam brought him up to the men at the fire just after we'd left to try to save Dad's Shropshires, and they and Mr. Morrison could hardly keep the men off him. He hid behind Sam, and cried and begged them to protect him. They said it was beastly."

"Rather!" said Harry. 'Where's he now?"

"Melbourne Goal. He got three years," said Jim. "I guest he's reflecting on the foolishness of using matches too freely!"

"By George!" said Wally, drawing a deep breath. "That was exciting, Jimmy!"

"Well, fishing isn't," responded Jim, pulling up his hook in disgust, an example followed by the other boys. "What'll we do?"

"I move," said Wally, standing on one leg on the log, "that this meeting do adjourn from this dead tree. And I move a hearty vote of thanks to Mr. Jim Linton for spinning a good yarn. Thanks to be paid immediately. There's mine, Jimmy!"

A resounding pat on the back startled Jim considerably, followed as it was by a second from Harry. The assaulted one fled along the log, and hurled mud furiously from the bank. The enemy followed closely, and shortly the painful spectacle might have been seen of a host lying flat on his face on the grass, while his guests, sitting on his back, bumped up and down to his extreme discomfort and the tune of "For He's a Jolly Good Fellow!"

CHAPTER 7

What Norah Found

NORAH, meanwhile, had been feeling somewhat "out of things." It was really more than human nature could be expected to bear that she should remain on the log with the three boys, while Jim told amazing yarns about her. Still it was decidedly lonesome in the jutting root of the old tree, looking fixedly at the water, in which placidly lay a float that had apparently forgotten that the first duty of a float is to bob.

Jim's voice, murmuring along in his lengthy recital, came to her softly, and she could see from her perch the interested faces of the two others. It mingled drowsily with the dull drone of bees in the ti-tree behind her, and presently Norah, to her disgust, found that she was growing drowsy too.

"This won't do!" she reflected, shaking herself. "If I go to sleep and tumble off this old root I'll startle away all the fish in the creek." She looked doubtfully at the still water, now and then rippled by the splash of a leaping fish. "No good when they jump like that," said Norah to herself. "I guess I'll go and explore."

She wound up her line quickly, and flung her bait to the lazy inhabitants of the creek as a parting gift. Then, unnoticed by the boys, she scrambled out of the tree and climbed up the bank, getting her blue riding-skirt decidedly muddy — not that Norah's free and independent soul had ever learned to tremble at the sight of muddy garments. She hid her fishing tackle in a stump, and made her way along the bank.

A little farther up she came across black Billy — a very cheerful Aborigine, seeing that he had managed to induce no less than nine blackfish to leave their watery bed.

"Oh, I say!" said Norah, round-eyed and envious. "How do you manage it, Billy? We can't catch one."

Billy grinned. He was a youth of few words.

"Plenty bob-um float," he explained lucidly. "Easy 'nuff. You try."

"No thanks," said Norah, though she hesitated for a moment. "I'm sick of trying — and I've no luck. Going to cook 'em for dinner, Billy?"

"Plenty!" assented Billy vigorously. It was his favourite word, and meant almost anything, and he rarely used another when he could make it suffice.

"That's good," said Norah approvingly, and Billy grinned from ear to ear. "I'm going for a walk, Billy. Tell Master Jim to coo-ee when lunch is ready."

"Plenty," said Billy intelligently.

Norah turned from the creek and entered the scrub. She loved the bush, and was never happier than when exploring its recesses. A born bush maid, she had never any difficulty about finding her way in the scrub, or of retracing her steps. The faculty of bushmanship must be born in you; if you have it not naturally, training very rarely gives it.

She rambled on aimlessly, noting, though scarcely conscious that she did so, the bush sights and scenes on either hand — clinging creepers and twining plants, dainty ferns, nestling in hollow trees, clusters of maiden-hair under logs; pheasants that hopped noiselessly in the shade, and a wallaby track in some moist, soft earth. Once she saw a carpet snake lying coiled in a tussock and, springing for a stick, she ran at it, but the snake was too quick for her and she was only in time to hit at its tail as it whisked down a hole. Norah wandered on, feeling disgusted with herself.

Suddenly she stopped in amazement.

She was on the edge of a small clear space, at the farther side of which was a huge blue-gum tree. Tall trees ringed it round, and the whole space was in deep shade. Norah stood rooted to the ground in surprise.

For at the foot of the big blue-gum was a strange sight, in that lonely place. It was nothing more or less than a small tent.

The flap of the tent was down, and there were no inhabitants to be seen; but all about were signs of occupation. A well-blackened billy hung from the ridge-pole. Close to the tent was a heap of dry sticks, and a little farther away the ashes of a fire still smouldered, and over them a blackened bough, supported by two forked sticks, showed that the billy had many times been boiled there. The little camp was all very neat and tidy. "It looks quite home-like," said Norah to herself.

As she watched, the flat of the tent was raised, and a very old man came out. He was so tall that he had to bend almost double in stooping under the canvas of the low tent. A queer old man, Norah thought him, as she drew back instinctively into the shadow of the trees. When he straightened himself he was wonderfully tall — taller even than Dad, who was over six feet. He wore no hat, and his hair and beard were very long, and as white as snow. Under bushy white eyebrows, a pair of bright blue eyes twinkled. Norah decided that they were nice eyes.

But he certainly was queer. His clothes would hardly have passed muster in Collins Street, and would even have attracted attention in Cunjee. He was dressed entirely in skins — wallaby skins, Norah guessed, though there was an occasional section that looked like possum. They didn't look bad, either, she thought — a kind of sleeved waistcoat, and loose trousers, that were met at the knee by roughly-tanned gaiters, or leggings. Still, the whole effect was startling.

The old man walked across to his fire and kneeling down, carefully raked away the ashes. Then he drew out a damper — Norah had never seen one before, but she knew immediately that it was a damper. It looked good, too — nicely risen, and brown, and it sent forth a fragrance that was decidedly appetising. The old man looked pleased. "Not half bad!" he said aloud, in a wonderfully deep voice, which sounded so amazing in the bush silence that Norah fairly jumped.

The old man raked the ashes together again, and placed some sticks on them, after which he brought over the billy, and hung it above the fire to boil. The fire quickly broke into a blaze, and he picked up the damper again, and walked slowly back to the tent, where he paused to blow the dust from the result of his cookery.

At this moment Norah became oppressed with a wild desire to sneeze. She fought against it frantically, nearly choking in her efforts to remain silent, while she wildly explored in her pockets for a non-existent handkerchief.

As the water bursts from the dam the more violently because of its imprisonment, so Norah's sneeze gained intensity and uproar from her efforts to repress it. It came —

"A—tish—oo—oo!"

The old man started violently. He dropped his damper and gazed round.

"What on earth's that?" he said. "Who's there?"

For a moment Norah hesitated. Should she run for her life? But a second's thought showed her no real reason why she should run. She was not in the least frightened, for it never occurred to Norah that anyone could wish to hurt her; and she had done nothing to make him angry. So she modestly emerged from behind a friendly tree and said meekly, "It's me."

" 'Me,' is it?" said the old man, in great astonishment. He stared hard at the little figure in the blue blouse and serge riding-skirt — at the merry face and the dark curls crowned by the

shady Panama hat. " 'Me,' " he repeated. " 'Me'
looks rather nice, I think. But what's she doing
here?"

"I was looking at you," Norah exclaimed.

"I won't be unpolite enough to mention that a
cat may look at a king," said the old man. "But
don't you know that no one comes here? No young
ladies in blue dresses and brown curls — only
wombats and wallabies, and ring-tailed possums
— and me. Not you-me, but me-me! How do you
account for being here?"

Norah laughed. She decided that she liked this
very peculiar old man, whose eyes twinkled so
brightly as he spoke.

"But I don't think you know," she said. "Quite
a lot of other people come here — this is Anglers'
Bend. At least, Anglers' Bend's quite close to your
camp. Why, only today there's Jim and the boys,
and black Billy, and me! We're not wallabies!"

"Jim — and the boys — and black Billy — and
me!" echoed the old man faintly. "Angels and
ministers of grace, defend us! And I thought I had
found the back of beyond, where I would never see
any one more civilised than a bunyip! But — I've
been here for three months, little lady, and have
never come across anyone. Are you sure you're
quite serious?"

"Quite," Norah answered. "Perhaps it was that
no one came across you, you know, because people
really do come here to fish. Dad and I camp here
sometimes, but we haven't been for more than
three months."

"Well, I must move, that's all," said the old man.
"I do like quiet — it's annoying enough to have to

dress up and go into a township now and then for stores. How do you like my clothes, by the way? I may as well have a feminine opinion while I have the chance."

"Did you make them yourself?" asked Norah.

"Behold how she fences!" said the old man. "I did indeed!"

"Then they do you proud!" said Norah solemnly.

The old man laughed.

"I shall prize your expression of opinion," he said. "May I ask the name of my visitor?"

"I'm Norah. Please, who are you?"

"That's a different matter," said the other, looking nonplussed. "I certainly had a name once, but I've quite forgotten it. I have an excellent memory for forgetting. Would you think I was a bunyip? I'd be delighted if you could!"

"I couldn't." Norah shook her head. "But I'll tell you what I think you are."

"Do."

"A hermit!"

The old man's face cleared.

"My dear Miss Norah," he said, "you've made a profound discovery. I am — I am — a hermit! Thank you very much. Being a hermit my resources are scanty, but may I hope that you will have lunch with me?"

"I can't, I'm afraid," said Norah, looking affectionately at the damper. "The boys will be looking for me, if I don't go back. Listen — there's Jim coo-eeing now!"

"And who may Jim be?" queried the Hermit, a trifle uneasily.

"Jim's my brother," Norah said. "He's fifteen,

and he's just splendid. Harry and Wally are his
two chums."

"Coo-ee! Coo-ee!"

Norah answered the call quickly and turned to
the Hermit, feeling a little apologetic.

"I had to call," she explained. "Jim would be
anxious. They want me for lunch." She hesitated.
"Won't you come too?" she asked timidly.

"I haven't eaten with my fellow-men for more
time than I'd care to reckon," said the Hermit. "I
don't know — will you let me alone afterwards?
Are they ordinary abominable boys?"

"Indeed, they're not!" said Norah indignantly.
"They won't come near you at all, if you don't want
them — but I know they'd be pleased if you came.
Do!"

"Coo-ee!"

"Jim's getting impatient, isn't he?" said the
hermit. "Well, Miss Norah, if you'll excuse my
attire I'll come. Shall I bring my damper?"

"Oh, please!" Norah cried. "We've never tasted
damper."

"I wish *I* hadn't," said the Hermit grimly. He
picked up the fallen cake. "Let us away!" he said,
"the banquet waits!"

During the walk through the scrub it occurred
to Norah once or twice to wonder if her companion
were really a little mad. He said such extra-
ordinary things, all in the most matter-of-fact tone
— but when she looked up at him his blue eyes
twinkled so kindly and merrily that she knew at
once he was all right, and she was quite certain
that she liked him very much.

The boys were getting impatient. Lunch was

ready, and when lunch has been prepared by Mrs. Brown, and supplemented by fresh blackfish, fried over a camp fire by black Billy, it is not a meal to be kept waiting. They were grouped round the table-cloth, in attitudes more suggestive of ease than elegance, when Norah and her escort appeared, and for once their manners deserted them. They gaped in silent amazement.

"Boys, this is The Hermit," said Norah, rather nervously. "I — I found him. He has a camp. He's come to lunch."

"I must apologise for my intrusion, I'm afraid," the hermit said. "Miss Norah was good enough to ask me to come. I — I've brought my damper!"

He exhibited the article half shyly, and the boys recovered themselves and laughed uncontrollably. Jim sprang to his feet. The Hermit's first words had told him that this was no common swagman that Norah had picked up.

"I'm very glad to see you, sir," he said, holding out his hand.

"Thank you," said the Hermit gravely. "You're Jim, aren't you? And I conclude that this gentleman is Harry, and this Wally? Ah, I thought so. Yes, I haven't seen so many people for ages. And black Billy! How are you, Billy?"

Billy retreated in great embarrassment.

"Plenty!" he murmured.

Everybody laughed again.

"Well," Jim said, "we're hungry, Norah. I hope you and — er — this gentleman are." Jim was concealing his bewilderment like a hero. "Won't you sit down and sample Billy's blackfish? He caught 'em all — we couldn't raise a bit between us — barring Wally's boot!"

"Did you catch a boot?" queried the Hermit of the blushing Wally. "Mine, I think — I can't congratulate you on your luck! If you like, after lunch, I'll show you a place where you could catch fish, if you only held the end of your finger in the water!"

"Good enough!" said Jim. "Thanks, awfully — we'll be jolly glad. Come on, Billy — trot out your frying-pan!"

Lunch began rather silently.

In their secret hearts the boys were rather annoyed with Norah.

"Why on earth," Jim reflected, "couldn't she have left the old chap alone? The party was all right without him — we didn't want anyone else — least of all an old oddity like this." And though the other boys were loyal to Norah, she certainly suffered a fall in their estimation, and was classed for the moment with the usual run of "girls who do rummy things."

However, the Hermit was a man of penetration and soon realised the state of the social barometer. His hosts, who did not look at all like quiet boys, were eating their blackfish in perfect silence, save for polite requests for bread or pepper, or the occasional courteous remark, "Chuck us the salt!"

Accordingly the Hermit exerted himself to please, and it would really have taken more than three crabby boys to resist him. He told the drollest stories, which sent everyone into fits of laughter, although he never laughed himself at all; and he talked about the bush, and told them of the queer animals he saw — having, as he said, unusually good opportunities for watching the bush inhabitants unseen. He knew where the lyrebirds danced, and had often crept silently through the scrub until he could command a view of the mound where these strange birds strutted and danced, and mimicked the other birds with life-like fidelity. He loved the birds very much, and never killed any of them, even when a pair of thievish magpies attacked his larder and pecked a damper into little bits when he was away fishing. Many of the birds were tame with him now, he said; they would hop about the camp and let him feed them; and he had a carpet snake that was quite a pet, which he offered to show them — an offer that broke down the last tottering barriers of the boys' reserve. Then there were his different methods of trapping animals, some of which were strange even to Jim, who was a trapper of much renown.

"Don't you get lonely sometimes?" Norah asked him.

The Hermit looked at her gravely.

"Sometimes," he said. "Now and then one feels that one would give something to hear a human voice again, and to feel a friend's hand-grip. Oh, there are times, Miss Norah, when I talk to myself — which is bad — or yarn to old Turpentine, my snake, just to hear the sound of words again. However, when these bad fits come upon me I know it's a sign that I must get the axe and go and chop down sufficient trees to make me tired. Then I go to sleep, and wake up quite a cheerful being once more!"

He hesitated.

"And there's one thing," he said slowly, "though it may be lonely here, there is no one to trouble you; no one to treat you badly, to be ungrateful or malicious; no bitter enemies, and no false friends, who are so much worse than enemies. The birds come and hop about me, and I know that it is because I like them and have never frightened them; old Turpentine slides his ugly head over my knees, and I know he doesn't care a button whether I have any money in my pocket, or whether I have to go out into the scrub to find my next meal! And that's far, far more than you can say of most human beings!"

He looked round on their grave faces, and smiled for the first time.

"This is uncommonly bad behaviour in a guest," he said cheerily. "To come to lunch, and regale one's host and hostess with a sermon! It's too bad. I ask your forgiveness, young people, and please forget all I said immediately. No, Miss Norah, I won't have any damper, thank you — after a three months' course of damper one looks with joy once more on bread. If Wally will favour me — I think the correct phrase is will you 'chuck me the butter?' " — whereat Wally "chucked" as desired, and the meal proceeded merrily.

CHAPTER 8

On a Log

LUNCH over, everyone seemed disinclined for action. The boys lay about on the grass, sleepily happy. Norah climbed into a tree, where the gnarled boughs made a natural arm-chair, and the Hermit propped his back against a rock and smoked a short black pipe with an air of perfect enjoyment. It was just hot enough to make one drowsy. Bees droned lazily, and from some shady gully the shrill note of a cricket came faintly to the ear. Only Billy had stolen down to the creek, to tempt the fish once more. They heard the dull "plunk" of his sinker as he flung it into a deep, still pool.

"Would you like to hear how I lost my boot?" queried the Hermit suddenly.

"Oh, please," said Norah.

The boys rolled over — that is to say Jim and Wally rolled over. Harry was fast asleep.

"Don't wake him," said the Hermit. But Wally's hat, skilfully thrown, had already caught the slumberer on the side of the head.

Harry woke up with surprising promptness, and returned the offending head-gear with force and directness. Wally caught it deftly and rammed it

over his eyes. He smiled underneath it at the
Hermit like a happy cherub.

"Now we're ready, sir," he said. "Hold your row,
Harry, the — this gentleman's going to spin us a
yarn. Keep awake if you can spare the time!"

"I'll spare the time to kick you!" growled the
indignant Harry.

"I don't know that you'll think it's much of a
yarn," the Hermit said hurriedly, entering the
breach to endeavour to allay further discussion —
somewhat to Jim's disappointment. "It's only the
story of a pretty narrow escape.

"I had gone out fishing one afternoon about a
month ago. It was a grand day for fishing — dull
and cloudy. The sun was about somewhere, but
you couldn't see anything of him, although you
could feel his warmth. I'd been off colour for a few
days, and had not been out foraging at all, and as
a result, except for damper, my larder was quite
empty.

"I went about a mile upstream. There's a
splendid place for fishing there. The creek widens,
and there's a still, deep pool, something like the
pool at the place you call Anglers' Bend, only I
think mine is deeper and stiller, and fishier! At
all events, I have never failed to get fish there.

"I fished from the bank for a while, with not
very good luck. At all events, it occurred to me
that I could better it if I went out upon a big log
that lay right across the creek — a tremendous
tree it must have been, judging by the size of the
trunk. You could almost ride across it, it's so wide
— if you had a circus pony, that is," added the
Hermit with a twinkle.

"So I gathered up my tackle, hung the fish I'd caught across a bough in the shade, and went out on the log, and here I had good luck at once. The fish bit just as soon as I put the bait into the water, and though a good many of them were small there were some very decent-sized ones amongst them. I threw the little chaps back, on the principle that —

> *Baby fish you throw away*
> *Will make good sport another day,*

and at last began to think I had caught nearly enough, even though I intended to salt some. However, just as I thought it was time to strike for camp, I had a tremendous bite. It nearly jerked the rod out of my hands!

" 'Hallo!' I said to myself, 'here's a whale!' I played him for a bit, for he was the strongest fish I ever had on a line in this country, and at last he began to tire, and I reeled the line in. It seemed quite a long time before I caught a glimpse of his lordship — a tremendous perch. I tell you I felt quite proud as his head came up out of the water.

"He was nearly up to the log, when he made a sudden, last leap in the air, and the quickness of it and his weight half threw me off my balance. I made a hurried step on the log, and my right foot slipped into a huge, gaping crack. It was only after I had made two or three ineffectual struggles to release it that I found I was stuck!

"Well, I didn't realise the seriousness of the position for a few minutes," the Hermit went on. "I could understand that I was wedged, but I certainly never dreamed that I could not, by dint of manoeuvring, wriggle my foot out of the crack. So I turned my attention to my big fish, and — standing in a most uncomfortable position — managed to land him; and a beauty he was, handsome as paint, with queer markings on his sides. I put him down carefully, and then tried to free myself.

"And I tried — and tried — and tried — until I was tired out, and stiff and hopeless. By that time it was nearly dark. After I had endeavoured unsuccessfully to get the boot clear, I unlaced it, and tried to get my foot out of it — but I was in a trifle too far for that, and try as I would, I could not get it free. The crack was rather on the side of the log. I could not get a straight pull. Hurt? Yes, of course it hurt — not more from the pinching of the log, which you may try any time by screwing your foot up in a vice, than from my own wild efforts to get clear. My foot and ankle were stiff and sore from my exertions long before I knocked off in despair. I might have tried to cut the wood away, had I not left my knife on the bank, where I was fishing first. I don't know that it would have done much good, anyhow.

"Well, I looked at the situation — in fact, I had been looking at it all the time. It wasn't a very cheering prospect, either. The more I pondered over it, the less chance I saw of getting free. I had done all I could towards that end; now it only remained to wait for something to 'turn up.' And I was quite aware that nothing was in the least likely to turn up, and also that in all probability I would wear out some time before the log did.

"Night came on, and I was as hungry as a
hunter — being a hunter, I knew just how hungry
that is. I hadn't anything to eat except raw fish,
and I wasn't quite equal to that yet. I had only
one pipe of tobacco too, and you may be sure I
made the most of that. I smoked it very, very
slowly, and I wouldn't like to say how long it
lasted.

"From time to time I made fresh attempts to
release my foot — all unavailing, and all the more
maddening because I could feel that my foot wasn't
much caught — only just enough to hold it. But
enough is as good as a feast! I felt that if I could
get a straight pull at it I might get it out, and
several times I nearly went head first into the
water, overbalancing myself in the effort to get
that straight pull. That wasn't a pleasant sen-
sation — not so bad, indeed, if one had got as far
as the water. But I pictured myself hanging from
the log with a dislocated ankle, and the prospect
was not inviting.

"So the night crept on. I grew deadly sleepy, but
of course I did not care to let myself go to sleep;
but worse than that was the stiffness, and the
cramp that tortured the imprisoned leg. You know
how you want to jump when you've got cramp?
Well, I wanted to jump at intervals of about a
minute all through that night, and instead, I was
more securely hobbled than any old horse I ever
saw. The mosquitoes worried me too. Altogether
it was not the sort of entertainment you would
select from choice!

"And then, just as day began to dawn, the
sleepiness got the better of me. I fought it

unavailingly; but at last I knew I could keep
awake no longer, and I shut my eyes.

"I don't know how long I slept — it couldn't have
been for any time, for it was not broad daylight
when I opened my eyes again. Besides, the
circumstances weren't the kind to induce calm and
peaceful slumber.

"I woke up with a start, and in my dreams I
seemed to hear myself crying out with pain — for
a spasm of cramp had seized me, and it was like
a red-hot iron thrust up my leg. I was only half
awake — not realising my position a bit. I made
a sudden spring, and the next moment off I went,
headlong!

"I don't suppose," said the Hermit reflectively,
poking a stem of grass down his pipe, "that I'll
ever lose the memory of the sudden, abject terror
of that moment. They say 'as easy as falling off a
log,' and it certainly doesn't take an able-bodied
man long to fall off one, as a rule; but it seemed
to me that I was hours and years waiting for the
jerk to come on my imprisoned foot. I'm sure I
lived through half a lifetime before it really came.

"Then it came — and I hardly felt it! There was
just a sudden pull — scarcely enough to hurt very
much, and the old boot yielded. Sole from upper,
it came clean away, and the pressure on my foot
alone wasn't enough to hold me. It was so
unexpected that I didn't realise I was free until I
struck the water, and went down right into the
mud at the bottom of the creek!

"That woke me up, I can assure you. I came up
choking and spluttering, and blinded with the mud
— I wouldn't like to tell you for a moment that it

was pleasant, but I can truthfully say I never was more relieved in my life. I struck out for the bank, and got out of the water, and then sat down on the grass and wondered why on earth I hadn't made up my mind to jump off that log before.

"I hadn't any boot left — the remainder had been kicked off as I swam ashore. I made my way along the log that had held me so fast all night, and there, wedged as tight as ever in the crack, was my old sole! It's there still — unless the mosquitoes have eaten it. I limped home with my fish, cleaned them, had a meal and went to bed — and I didn't get up until next day, either!

"And so, Mr. Wally, I ventured to think that it was my boot that you landed this morning," the Hermit said gravely. "I don't grudge it to you; I can't say I ever wish to see it again. You" — magnanimously — "may have it for your very own!"

"But I chucked it back again!" blurted out Wally, amidst a roar of laughter from Jim and Harry at his dismayed face.

"I forgive you!" said the Hermit, joining the laugh. "I admit it was a relic which didn't advertise its own fame."

"I guess you'd never want to see it again," Jim said. "That was a pretty narrow escape — if your foot had been in just a bit further you might have been hanging from that old log now!"

"That was my own idea all that night," observed the Hermit, "and then Wally wouldn't have caught any more than the rest of you this morning! And that reminds me, I promised to show you a good fishing-place. Don't you think, if you've had enough of my prosy yarning, that we'd better make a start?"

The party gathered itself up with alacrity from the grass. Lines were hurriedly examined, and the bait tin, when investigated, proved to contain an ample supply of succulent grubs and other dainties calculated to temp the most fastidious of fish.

"All ready?" said the Hermit.

"Hold on a minute," Jim said. "I'll let Billy know where we're going."

Billy was found fishing stolidly from a log. Three blackfish testified to his skill with the rod, at which Wally whistled disgustedly and Norah laughed.

"No good to be jealous of Billy's luck," she said. "He can always get fish, when nobody else can find even a nibble. Mrs. Brown says he's got the light hand like hers for pastry."

The Hermit laughed.

"I like Mrs. Brown's simile," he said. "If that was her pastry in those turnovers at lunch, Miss Norah, I certainly agree that she has 'the light hand.' "

"Mrs. Brown's like the cook in *The Ingoldsby Legends*, Dad says," Norah remarked.

"What," said the Hermit —

> *"For soups and stews, and French ragouts,*
> *Nell Cook is famous still —?"*
> *"She'd make them even of old shoes*
> *She had such wondrous skill!"*

finished Norah delightedly. "However did you know, Mr. Hermit?"

The Hermit laughed, but a shade crossed his brow. "I used to read the *Legends* with a dear old friend many years before you were born, Miss Norah," he said gravely. "I often wonder whether he still reads them."

"Ready?" Jim interrupted, springing up the bank. "Billy understands about feeding the ponies. Don't forget, mind, Billy."

"Plenty!" quoth Billy, and the party went on its way.

The Hermit led them rapidly over logs and fallen trees, up and down gullies, and through tangles of thickly growing scrub. Once or twice it occurred to Jim that they were trusting very confidingly to this man, of whom they knew absolutely nothing; and a faint shade of uneasiness crossed his mind. He felt responsible, as the eldest of the youngsters, knowing that his father had placed him in charge, and that he was expected to exercise a certain amount of caution. Still it was hard to fancy anything wrong, looking at the Hermit's serene face, and the trusting way in which Norah's brown little hand was placed in his strong grasp. The other boys were quite unconscious of any uncomfortable ideas, and Jim finally dismissed his fears as uncalled for.

"I thought," said the Hermit, suddenly turning, "of taking you to see my camp as we went, but on second thoughts I decided that it would be better to get straight to work, as you young people want some fish, I suppose, to take home. Perhaps we can look in at my camp as we come back. It's not far from here."

"Which way do you generally go to the river?" Norah asked.

"Why, any way," the Hermit answered. "Generally in this direction. Why do you ask, Miss Norah?"

"I was wondering," Norah said. "We haven't crossed or met a single track."

The Hermit laughed.

"No," he said, "I take very good care not to leave tracks if I can avoid it. You see, I'm a solitary fellow, Miss Norah, and prefer, as a rule, to keep to myself. Apart from that, I often leave camp for the greater part of the day when I'm fishing or hunting, and I've no wish to point out the way to my domain to any wanderers. Not that I've much to lose, still there are some things. Picture my harrowed feelings were I to return some evening and find my beloved frying-pan gone!"

Norah laughed.

"It would be awful," she said.

"So I planned my camp very cunningly," continued the Hermit, "and I can tell you it took some planning to contrive it so that it shouldn't be too easily visible."

"Well, it isn't from the side I came on it." Norah put in. "I never dreamed of anything being there until I was right on the camp. It did surprise me!"

"And me," said the Hermit drily. "Well that is how I tried to arrange camp, and you could be within a dozen yards of it on any side without imagining that any of it was near."

"But surely you must have made some sort of a track leading away from it," said Jim, "unless you fly out!"

The Hermit laughed.

"I'll show you later how I manage that," he said.

The bush grew denser as the little party, led by the Hermit, pushed along, and Jim was somewhat surprised at the easy certainty with which their guide led the way, since there was no sign of a track. Being a silent youth, he held his tongue on the matter; but Wally was not so reserved.

"However d'you find your way along here?" he asked. "I don't even know whether we're near the creek or not."

"If we kept still a moment you'd know," the Hermit said. "Listen!" He held up his hand and they all stood still. There came faintly to his ears a musical splash of water.

"There's a little waterfall just in there," the Hermit said, "nothing much, unless the creek is very low, and then there is a greater drop for the water. How do I know the way? Why, I feel it mostly, and if I couldn't feel it, there are plenty of landmarks. Every big tree is as good as a signpost once you know the way a bit, and I've been along here pretty often, so there's nothing in it, you see, Wally."

"Do you like the bush, Mr. Hermit?" Norah asked.

The Hermit hesitated.

"Sometimes I hate it, I think, Miss Norah," he said, "when the loneliness of it comes over me, and all the queer sounds of it bother me and keep me awake. Then I realise that I'm really a good way from anywhere, and I get what are familiarly called the blues. However, that's not at all times, and indeed mostly I love it very much, its great quietness and its beauty; and then it's so companionable, though perhaps you're a bit young to understand that. Anyhow, I have my mates, not only old Turpentine, my snake, but others — wallabies that have come to recognise me as harmless, for I never hunt anywhere near home, the laughing jackasses, two of them, that come and guffaw to me every morning, the pheasants that I watch capering and strutting on the logs hidden in the scrub. Even the plants become friends; there are creepers near my camp that I've watched from babyhood, and more than one big tree with which I've at least a nodding acquaintance!"

He broke off suddenly.

"Look, there's a friend of mine!" he said gently.

They were crossing a little gully, and a few yards on their right a big wallaby sat staring at them, gravely inquisitive. It certainly would not have been human nature if Jim had not longed for a gun; but the wallaby was evidently quite ignorant of such a thing, and took them all in with his cool stare. At length Wally sneezed violently, whereat the wallaby started, regarded the disturber of his peace with an alarmed air, and finally bounded off into the scrub.

"There you go!" said the Hermit good-humouredly, "scaring my poor beastie out of his wits."

"Couldn't help it," mumbled Wally.

"No, a sneeze will out, like truth, won't it?" the Hermit laughed. "That's how Miss Norah announced herself to me today. I might never have known she was there if she hadn't obligingly sneezed! I hope you're not getting colds, children!" the Hermit added, with mock concern.

"Not much!" said Wally and Norah in a breath.

"Just after I came here," said the Hermit, "I was pretty short of tucker, and it wasn't a good time for fishing, so I was dependent on my gun for most of my provisions. So one day, feeling much annoyed after a breakfast of damper and jam, I took the gun and went off to stock up the larder.

"I went a good way without any luck. There didn't seem anything to shoot in all the bush, though you may be sure I kept my eyes about me. I was beginning to grow disheartened. At length I made my way down to the creek. Just as I got near it, I heard a whirr-r-r over my head, and looking up, I saw a flock of wild duck. They seemed to pause a moment, and then dropped downwards. I couldn't see where they alighted, but of course I knew it must be in the creek.

"Well, I didn't pause," said the Hermit. "I just made my way down to the creek as quickly as ever I could, remaining noiseless at the same time. Ducks are easily scared, and I knew my hopes of dinner were poor if these chaps saw me too soon.

"So I sneaked down. Pretty soon I got a glimpse of the creek, which was very wide at that point, and fringed with weeds. The ducks were calmly swimming on its broad surface, a splendid lot of them, and I can assure you a very tempting sight to a hungry man.

"However, I didn't waste time in admiration. I couldn't very well risk a shot from where I was, it was a bit too far, and the old gun I had wasn't very brilliant. So I crept along, crawled down a bank, and found myself on a flat that ran to the water's edge, where reeds, growing thickly, screened me from the ducks' sight.

"That was simple enough. I crawled across this flat, taking no chances, careless of mud, and wet, and sword grass, which isn't the nicest thing to crawl among at any time, as you can imagine; it's absolutely merciless to face and hands."

"And jolly awkward to stalk ducks in," Jim commented. "The rustle would give you away in no time."

The Hermit nodded.

"Yes," he said, "that's its worst drawback, or was, on this occasion. It certainly did rustle; however, I crept very slowly, and the ducks were kind enough to think I was the wind stirring in the reeds. At any rate, they went on swimming and feeding quite peacefully. I got a good look at them through the fringe of reeds, and then, like a duffer, although I had a good enough position, I must try and get a better one.

"So I crawled a little farther down the bank, trying to reach a knoll which would give me a fine sight of the game, and at the same time form a convenient rest for my gun. I had almost reached it when the sad thing happened. A tall, spear-like reed, bending over, gently and intrusively tickled my nose, and without the slightest warning, and very greatly to my own amazement, I sneezed violently.

"If I was amazed, what were the ducks! The sneeze was so unmistakably human, so unspeakably violent. There was one wild whirr of wings, and my ducks scrambled off the placid surface of the water like things possessed. I threw up my gun and fired wildly; there was not time for deliberate taking of aim, with the birds already half over the ti-tree at the other side."

"Did you get any?" Jim asked.

"One duck," said the Hermit sadly. "And even for him I had to swim; he obligingly chose a watery grave just to spite me, I believe. He wasn't much of a duck either. After I had stripped and swum for him, dressed again, prepared the duck, cooked him, and finally sat down to dinner, there was so little on him that he only amounted to half a meal, and was tough at that!"

"So was your luck," observed Wally.

"Uncommonly tough," agreed the Hermit. "However, these things are the fortunes of war, and one has to put up with them, grin, and play the game. It's surprising how much tougher things look if you once begin to grumble. I've had so much bad luck in the bush that I've really got quite used to it."

"How's that?" asked Harry.

"Why," said the Hermit, "if it wasn't one thing, it was mostly another. I beg your pardon, Miss Norah, let me help you over this log. I've had my tucker stolen again and again, several times by birds, twice by swaggies, and once by a couple of black fellows pilgrimaging through the bush. I don't know whither they happened on my camp, and helped themselves; I reckoned myself very lucky that they only took food, though I've no doubt they would have taken more if I hadn't arrived on the scene in the nick of time and scared them almost out of their wits."

"How did you do that?" asked Norah. "Tell us about it, Mr. Hermit!"

The Hermit smiled down at Norah's eager face.

"Oh, that's hardly a yarn, Miss Norah," he said, his eyes twinkling in a way that made them look astonishingly young, despite his white hair and his wrinkles. "That was only a small happening, though it capped a day of bad luck. I had been busy in camp all the morning, cooking, and had laid in quite a supply of tucker, for me. I'd cooked some wild duck, and roasted a hare, boiled a most splendid plum-duff, and finally baked a big damper, and I can tell you I was patting myself on the back because I need not do any more cooking for nearly a week, unless it were fish — I'm not a cook by nature, and pretty often go hungry rather than prepare a meal.

"After dinner I thought I'd go down to the creek and try my luck — it was a perfect day for fishing, still and grey. So I dug some worms — and broke my spade in doing so — and started off.

"The promise of the day held good. I went to my favourite spot, and the fish just rushed me — the worms must have been very tempting, or else the fish larder was scantily supplied. At any rate, they bit splendidly, and soon I grew fastidious, and was picking out and throwing back any that weren't quite large enough. I fished from the old log over the creek, and soon had a pile of fish, and grew tired of the sport. I was sleepy, too, through hanging over the fire all the morning. I kept on fishing mechanically, but it was little more than holding my bait in the water, and I began nodding and dozing, leaning back on the broad old log.

"I didn't think I had really gone to sleep, though I suppose I must have done so, because I dreamed a kind of half-waking dream. In it I saw a snake that crept and crept nearer and nearer to me until I could see its wicked eyes gleaming, and though I tried to get away, I could not. It came on and on, until it was quite near, and I was feeling highly uncomfortable in my dream. At last I made a great effort, flung out my hand towards a stick, and, with a yell, woke up, to realise that I had struck something cold, and clammy, and wet. What it was I couldn't be certain for an instant, until I heard a dull splash, and then I knew. I had swept my whole string of fish into the water below!

"Oh, yes, I said things — who wouldn't? I was too disgusted to fish any more, and the nightmare having thoroughly roused me. I gathered up my tack and made tracks for home, feeling considerably annoyed with myself.

"You must know I've a private entrance into my camp. It's a track no one would suspect of being a track, and by its aid I can approach noiselessly. I've got into a habit of always sneaking back to camp — just in case anyone should be there. This afternoon I came along quietly, more from force of habit than from any real idea of looking out for intruders. But halfway along it a sound pulled me up suddenly. It was the sound of a voice.

"When you haven't heard anyone speak for a good many months, the human voice has quite a startling effect upon you — or even the human sneeze, Miss Norah!" added the Hermit, with a twinkle. "I stopped short and listened with all my might. Presently the voice came again, low and guttural, and I knew it for a native's.

"The conviction didn't fill me with joy, as you may imagine. I stole forward, until by peeping through the bushes I gained a view of the camp — and was rewarded with the spectacle of two blacks quite at home, one in the act of stuffing my cherished roast hare into a dirty bag, the other just taking a huge bite out of my damper!

"The sight, as you may imagine, didn't fill me with joy. From the bulges in my black visitors' bag I gathered that the ducks had preceded the hare; and even as I looked, the gentleman with the damper relaxed his well-meant efforts, and thrust it, too, into the bag. Then they put down the bag and dived into the tent, and I heard rustlings and low-toned remarks that breathed satisfaction. I reckoned it was time to step in.

"Luckily, my gun was outside the tent — indeed I never leave it inside, but have a special hiding-place for it under a handy log, for fear of stray marauders overhauling my possessions. A gun is a pretty tempting thing to most men, and since my duck-shooting failure I had treated myself to a new double-barrel — a beauty.

"I crept to the log, drew out both guns, and then retired to the bushes — a little uncertain, to tell the truth, what to do, for I hadn't any particular wish to murder my dusky callers; and at the same time, had to remember that they were two to one, and would be unhampered by any feeling of chivalry, if we did come to blows. I made up my mind to try to scare them — and suddenly I raised the most horrible, terrifying, unearthly yell I could think of, and at the same time fired both barrels of one gun quickly in the air!

"The effect was instantaneous. There was one howl of horror, and the black fellows darted out of the tent! They almost cannoned into me — and you know I must look a rum chap in these furry clothes and cap, with my grandfatherly white beard! At all events, they seemed to think me so, for at sight of me they both yelled in terror, and bolted away as fast as their legs could carry them. I cheered the parting guests by howling still more heartily, and firing my two remaining barrels over their heads as they ran. They went as swiftly as a motor-car disappears from view — I believe they reckoned they'd seen the bunyip. I haven't seen a trace of them since.

"They'd had a fine time inside the tent. Everything I possessed had been investigated, and one or two books badly torn — the wretches!" said the Hermit ruefully. "My clothes (I've a few garments besides these beauties, Miss Norah) had been pulled about, my few papers scattered wildly, and even my bunk stripped of blankets, which lay rolled up ready to be carried away. There wasn't a single one of my poor possessions that had escaped notice, except, of course, my watch and money, which I keep carefully buried. I counted myself very lucky to get off as lightly as I did — had I returned an hour later none of my goods and chattels would have been left."

"What about the tucker?" Harry asked. "Did they get away with the bag they'd stowed it in?"

"Not they!" said the Hermit, "they were far too scared to think of bags or tucker. They almost fell over it in their efforts to escape, but neither of them thought of picking it up. It was hard luck for them, after they'd packed it so carefully."

"Is that how you looked at it?" Jim asked, laughing.

"Well — I tried to," said the Hermit, laughing in his turn. "Sometimes it was pretty hard work — and I'll admit that for the first few days my own misfortunes were uppermost."

"Poor you!" said Norah.

"Oh, I wasn't so badly off," said the hermit. "They'd left me the plum-duff, which was hanging in its billy from a bough. Lots of duff — I had it morning, noon and night, until I found something fresh to cook — and I haven't made duff since. And here we are at the creek!"

CHAPTER 9

Fishing

THE party had for some time been walking near the creek, so close to it that it was within sound, although they seldom got a glimpse of water, save where the ti-tree scrub on the bank grew thinner or the light wind stirred an opening in its branches. Now, however, the Hermit suddenly turned, and although the others failed to perceive any tracks or landmark, he led them quickly through the scrub belt to the bank of the creek beyond.

It was indeed an ideal place for fishing. A deep, quiet pool, partly shaded by big trees, lay placid and motionless, except for an occasional ripple, stirred by a light puff of wind. An old wattle tree grew on the bank, its limbs jutting out conveniently, and here Jim and Wally ensconced themselves immediately, and turned their united attention to business. For a time no sound was heard save the dull "plunk" of sinkers as the lines, one by one, were flung into the water.

The Hermit did not fish. He had plenty at his camp, he said, and fishing for fun had lost its excitement, since he fished for a living most days of the week. So he contented himself with advising the others where to throw in, and finally sat down on the grass near Norah.

A few minutes passed. Then Jim jerked his line hurriedly and began to pull in with a feverish expression. It lasted until a big black fish made its appearance, dangling from the hook, and then it was suddenly succeeded by a look of intense disgust, as a final wriggle released the prisoner, which fell back with a splash into the water.

"Well, I'm blessed!" said Jim wrathfully.

"Hard luck!" said Harry.

"Try again, Jimmy, and stick to him this time," counselled Wally, in a fatherly tone.

"Oh, you shut up," Jim answered, re-baiting his hook. "I didn't catch an old boot, anyhow!" — which pertinent reflection had the effect of silencing Wally, amidst mild mirth on the part of the other members of the expedition.

Scarcely a minute more, and Norah pulled sharply at her line and began to haul in rapidly.

"Got a whale?" inquired Jim.

"Something like it!" Norah pulled wildly.

"Hang on!"

"Stick to him!"

"Mind your eye!"

"Don't get your line tangled!"

"Want any help, Miss Norah?"

"No, thanks." Norah was almost breathless. A red spot flamed in each cheek.

Slowly the line came in. Presently it gave a sudden jerk, and was tugged back quickly, as the fish made another run for liberty. Norah uttered an exclamation, quickly suppressed, and caught it sharply, pulling strongly.

Ah — he was out! A big, handsome perch, struggling and dancing in the air at the end of the line. Shouts broke from the boys as Norah landed her prize safely on the bank.

"Well done, Miss Norah," said the Hermit warmly. "That's a beauty — as fine a perch as I've seen in this creek."

"Oh, isn't he a splendid fellow!" Norah cried, surveying the prey with dancing eyes. "I'll have him for Dad, anyhow, even if I don't catch another."

"Yes, Dad's breakfast's all right," laughed the Hermit. "But don't worry, you'll catch more yet. See, there goes Harry."

There was a shout as Harry, with a scientific flourish of his rod, hauled a small black fish from its watery bed.

"Not bad for a beginning!" he said, grinning. "But not a patch on yours, Norah!"

"Oh, I had luck," Norah said. "He's really is a beauty, isn't he? I think he must be the grandfather of all the perches."

"If that's so," said Jim, beginning to pull in, with an expression of "do or die" earnestness, "I reckon I've got the grandmother on now!"

A storm of advice hurtled about Jim as he tugged at his line.

"Hurry up, Jim!"

"Go slow!"

"There — he's getting off again!"

"So are you!" said the ungrateful recipient of the counsel, pulling hard.

"Only a boot, Jim — don't worry!"

"Gammon! — it's a shark! — look at his worried expression!"

"I'll 'shark' you, young Harry!" grunted Jim. "Mind your eye — there he comes!" and expressions of admiration broke from the scoffers as a second splendid perch dangled in the air and was landed high and dry — or comparatively so — in the branches of the wattle tree.

"Is he as big as yours, Norah?" queried Jim a minute later, tossing his fish down on the grass close to his sister and the Hermit.

Norah laid the two fishes alongside.

"Not quite," she announced. "Mine's about an inch longer, and a bit fatter."

"Well, that's all right," Jim said. "I said it was the grandmother I had — yours is certainly the grandfather! I'm glad you got the biggest, old girl." They exchanged a friendly smile.

A yell from Wally intimated that he had something on his hook and with immense pride he flourished in the air a diminutive blackfish — so small that the Hermit proposed to use it for bait, a suggestion promptly declined by the captor, who hid his catch securely in the fork of two branches, before re-baiting his hook. Then Harry pulled out a fine perch, and immediately afterwards Norah caught a blackfish; and after that the fun waxed fast and furious, the fish biting splendidly, and all hands being kept busy. An hour later Harry shook the last worm out of the bait tin and dropped it into the water on his hook, where it immediately was seized by a perch of very tender years.

"Get back and grow till next year," advised

Harry, detaching the little prisoner carefully, the hook having caught lightly in the side of its mouth. "I'll come for you next holidays!" and he tossed the tiny fellow back into the water. "That's our last scrap of bait, you chaps," he said, beginning to wind up his line.

"I've been fishing with an empty hook for I don't know how long," said Jim, hauling up also. "These beggars have nibbled my bait off and carefully dodged the hook."

"Well, we've plenty, haven't we?" Norah said. "Just look what a splendid pile of fish!"

"They take a bit of beating, don't they?" said Jim. "That's right, Wal, pull him up!" — as Wally hauled in another fine fish. "We couldn't carry more if we had 'em."

"Then it's a good thing my bait's gone, too!" laughed Norah, winding up. "Haven't we had a most lovely time!"

Jim produced a roll of canvas which turned out to be two sugar bags, and in these carefully bestowed the fish, sousing the whole thoroughly in the water. The boys gathered up the lines and tackle and "planted" the rods conveniently behind a log, "to be ready for next time," they said.

"Well, we've had splendid sport, thanks to you, sir," Jim said, turning to the Hermit, who stood looking on at the preparations, a benevolent person, "something between Father Christmas and Robinson Crusoe," as Norah whispered to Harry. "We certainly wouldn't have got on half as well if we'd stayed where we were."

"Oh, I don't know," the Hermit answered. "Yours is a good place — I've often caught plenty of fish there — only not to be relied on as this pool is. I've really never known this particular spot fail — the fish seem to live in it all the year round. However, I'm glad you've had decent luck — it's not a bit jolly to go home empty-handed, I know. And now, what's the next thing to be done? The afternoon's getting on — don't you think it's time you came to pay me a visit at the camp?"

"Oh, yes, please!" Norah cried.

Jim hesitated.

"We'd like awfully to see your camp, if — if it's not any bother to you," he said.

"Not the least in the world," the Hermit said. "Only I can't offer you any refreshment. I've nothing but cold possum and tea, and the possum's an acquired taste, I'm afraid. I've no milk for the tea, and no damper, either!"

"By George!" said Jim remorsefully. "Why, we ate all your damper at lunch!"

"I can easily manufacture another," the Hermit said, laughing. "I'm used to the process. Only I don't suppose I could get it done soon enough for afternoon tea."

"We've loads of tucker," Jim said. "Far more than we're likely to eat. Milk, too. We meant to boil the billy again before we start for home."

"I'll tell you what," Norah said, struck by a brilliant idea. "Let's coo-ee for Billy, and when he comes send him back for our things. Then if — if Mr. Hermit likes, we could have tea at his camp."

"Why, that's a splendid notion," the Hermit cried. "I'm delighted that you thought of it, Miss Norah, although I'm sorry my guests have to supply their own meal! It doesn't seem quite the

thing — but in the bush, polite customs have to
fall into disuse. I only keep up my own good
manners by practising on old Turpentine, my
snake! However, if you're so kind as to overlook
my deficiencies, and make them up yourselves, by
all means let us come along and coo-ee for sweet
William!"

He shouldered one of the bags of fish as he
spoke, disregarding a protest from the boys. Jim
took the second, and they set out for the camp.

Their way led for some time along the track by
which they had come, if "track" it might be called.
Certainly, the Hermit trod it confidently enough,
but the others could only follow in his wake, and
wonder by what process he found his way so
quickly through the thick bush.

About half a mile along the creek the Hermit
suddenly turned off almost at right angles, and
struck into the scrub. The children followed him
closely, keeping as nearly at his heels as the
nature of the path would permit.

Norah found it not very pleasant. The Hermit
went at a good rate, swinging over the rough
ground with the sure-footed ease of one accustomed to the scrub and familiar with the path.
The boys, unhampered by skirts and long hair,
found no great difficulty in keeping up with him,
but the small maiden of the party, handicapped
by her clothes, to say nothing of being youngest
of them all, plodded along in the rear, catching on
sarsaparilla vines and raspberry tangles, plunging
head first through masses of dogwood, and getting
decidedly the worse of the journey.

Harry was the first to notice that Norah was

falling "into the distance," as he put it, and he ran back to her immediately.

"Poor old kid!" he said shamefacedly. "I'd no idea you were having such a beast of a time. Sorry, Norah!" His polite regrets were cut short by Norah's catching her foot in a creeper and falling bodily upon him.

"Thank you," said Harry, catching her deftly. "Delighted, I'm sure, ma'am! It's privilege to catch anyone like you. Come on, old girl, and I'll clear the track for you."

A little farther on the Hermit had halted, looking a trifle guilty.

"I'm really sorry, Miss Norah," he said, as Norah and Harry made their way up to the waiting group. "I didn't realise I was going at such a pace. We'll make haste more slowly."

He led the way, pausing now and again to make it easier for the little girl, holding the bushes aside and lifting her bodily over several big logs and sharp watercourses. Finally he stopped.

"I think if you give Billy a call now, Jim," he said, "he won't have much difficulty in finding us."

To the children it seemed an utter impossibility that Billy should ever find them, though they said nothing, and Jim obediently lifted up his voice and coo-ee'd in answer to the Hermit's words. For himself, Jim was free to confess he had quite lost his bearings, and the other boys were as much at sea as if they had suddenly been dropped down at the North Pole. Norah alone had an idea that they were not far from their original camping-place; an idea which was confirmed when a long "Ai-i-i!"

came in response to Jim's shout, sounding
startlingly near at hand.

"Master Billy has been making his way along
the creek," commented the Hermit. "He's no
distance off. Give him another call."

"Here!" Jim shouted. Billy answered again, and
after a few more exchanges, the bushes parted and
revealed black Billy, somewhat out of breath.

"Scoot back to camp, Billy," Jim ordered. "Take
these fish and soak 'em in the creek, and bring
back all our tucker — milk and all. Bring it —
Where'll he bring it, sir?" to the Hermit.

"See that tall tree, broken with the bough
dangling?" the Hermit asked, pointing some
distance ahead. Billy nodded. "Come back to that
and coo-ee, and we'll answer you."

"Plenty!" said Billy, shouldering the bags of fish,
and departing at a run. Billy had learnt early the
futility of wasting words.

"Come along," said the Hermit, laughing.

He turned off into the scrub, and led the way
again, taking, it seemed to Norah, rather a
roundabout path. At length he stopped short, near
a dense clump of dogwood.

"My back door," he said politely.

They stared about them. There was no sign of
any door at all, nor even of any footprints or marks
of traffic. The scrub was all about them; everything was very still and quiet in the afternoon
bush.

"Well, you've got us beaten and no mistake!"
Jim laughed, after they had peered fruitlessly
about. "Unless you camp in the air, I don't see —"

"Look here," said the Hermit.

He drew aside a clump of dogwood, and revealed the end of an old log — a huge tree-trunk that had long ago been a forest monarch, but having fallen, now stretched its mighty length more than a hundred feet along the ground. It was very broad and the uppermost side was flat, and here and there bore traces of caked, dry mud that showed where a boot had rested. The dogwood walled it closely on each side.

"That's my track home," the Hermit said. "Let me help you up, Miss Norah." He sprang up on the log as he spoke, and extended a hand to Norah, who followed him lightly. Then the Hermit led the way along the log, which was quite broad enough to admit of a wheelbarrow being drawn down its length. He stopped where the butt of the old tree, rising above the level of the trunk, barred the view, and pulling aside the dogwood, showed rough steps, cut in the side of the log.

"Down here, Miss Norah."

In a moment they were all on the ground beside him — Wally, disdaining the steps, having sprung down, and unexpectedly measured his length on the earth, to the accompaniment of much chaff. He picked himself up, laughing more than any of them, just as Norah popped her head through the scrub that surrounded them, and exclaimed delightedly —

"Why, here's the camp."

"I say," Jim said, following the Hermit into the little clearing, "You're well planted here!"

The space was not very large — a roughly circular piece of ground, ringed round with scrub, in which big gum trees reared their lofty heads.

A wattle tree stood in the centre, from its boughs dangling a rough hammock, made of sacking, while a water bag hung from another convenient branch. The Hermit's little tent was pitched at one side; across the clearing was the rude fireplace that Norah had seen in the morning. Everything, though rough enough, was very clean and tidy, with a certain attempt at comfort.

The Hermit laughed.

"Yes, I'm pretty well concealed," he agreed. "You might be quite close to the camp and never dream that it existed. Only bold explorers like Miss Norah would have hit upon it from the side where she appeared to me this morning, and my big log saves me the necessity of having a beaten track home. I try, by getting on it at different points, to avoid a track to the log, although, should a foot-mark lead anyone to it, the intruder would never take the trouble to walk down an old bush-hung tree-trunk, apparently for no reason. So that I feel fairly secure about my home and my belongings when I plan a fishing expedition or an excursion that takes me any distance away."

"Well, it's a good idea," Jim said. "Of course, a beaten track to your camp would be nothing more or less than an invitation to any swaggie or black fellow to follow it up."

"That's what I thought," the Hermit said, "and very awkward it would have been for me, seeing that one can't very well put a padlock on a tent, and that all my belongings are portable. Not that there's anything of great value. I have a few papers I wouldn't care to lose, a watch and a little money — but they're all safely buried in a cash-

box with a good lock. The rest I have to chance,
and, as I told you, I've so far been pretty lucky in
repelling invaders. There's not much traffic round
here, you know!"

Jim and Norah laughed. "Not much," they said,
nodding.

"My tent's not large," the Hermit said, leading
the way to that erection, which was securely and
snugly pitched with its back door (had there been
one) against the trunk of a huge dead tree. It was
a comparatively new tent, with a good fly, and was
watertight, its owner explained, in all weathers.
The flap was elaborately secured by many strings,
tied with wonderful and fearful knots.

"It must take you a long time to untie those
chaps every day," said Wally.

"It would," said the Hermit, "if I did untie them.
They're only part of my poor little scheme for
discouraging intruders, Master Wally." He slipped
his fingers inside the flap and undid a hidden
fastening, which opened the tent without dis-
arranging the array of intricate knots.

"A fellow without a knife might spend quite a
while in untying all those," said the Hermit. "He'd
be rather disgusted, on completing the job, to find
they had no bearing on the real fastening of the
tent. And perhaps by that time I might be home!"

The interior of the tent was scrupulously tidy
and very plain. A hastily put up bunk was covered
with blue blankets, and boasted a sacking pillow.
From the ridge-pole hung a candlestick, roughly
fashioned from a knot of wood, and the furniture
was completed by a rustic table and chair, made
from branches, and showing considerable

ingenuity in their fashioning. Wallaby skins thrown over the chair and upon the floor lent a look of comfort to the tiny dwelling; and a further touch of homeliness was given by many pictures cut from illustrated papers and fastened to the canvas walls. The fly of the tent projected some distance in front, and formed a kind of verandah, beneath which a second rustic seat stood, as well as a block of wood that bore a tin dish, and evidently did duty as a washstand. Several blackened billies hung about the camp, with a frying-pan that bore marks of long and honourable use.

The children surveyed this unusual home with much curiosity and interest, and the boys were loud in their praises of the chairs and tables. The Hermit listened to their outspoken comments with a benevolent look, evidently pleased with their approval, and soon Jim and he were deep in a discussion of bush carpentry — Jim, as Wally said, reckoning himself something of an artist in that line, and being eager for hints. Meanwhile the other boys and Norah wandered about the camp, wondering at the completeness that had been arrived at with so little material, and at its utter loneliness and isolation.

"A man might die here half a dozen times, and no one be any the wiser." Wally said. "It wouldn't like it myself."

"Once would be enough for most chaps," Harry grinned.

"Oh, get out! you know what I mean," retorted Wally. "You chaps are never satisfied unless you're pulling my leg — it's a wonder I don't limp! But seriously, what a jolly rum life for a man to choose."

"He's an educated chap, too," Harry said. "Talks like a book when he likes. I wonder what on earth he's doing it for?"

They had dropped their voices instinctively, and had moved away from the tent.

"He's certainly not the ordinary swaggie," Norah said slowly.

"Not by a good bit," Wally agreed. "Why, he can talk like our English master at school! Perhaps he's hiding."

"Might be," Harry said. "You never can tell — he's certainly keen enough on getting away from people."

"He's chosen a good place, then."

"Couldn't be better. I wonder if there's anything in it — if he really has done anything and doesn't want to be found?"

"I never heard such bosh!" said Norah indignantly. "One would think he really looked wicked, instead of being such a kind old chap. D'you think he's gone and committed a murder, or robbed a bank, or something like that? I wonder you're not afraid to be in his camp!"

The boys stared in amazement.

"Whew-w-w!" whistled Wally.

Harry flushed a little.

"Oh, steady, Norah!" he protested. "We really didn't mean to hurt your feelings. It was only an idea. I'll admit he doesn't look a hardened sinner."

"Well, you shouldn't have such ideas," Norah said stoutly; "he's a great deal too nice, and look how kind he's been to us! If he chooses to plant himself in the bush, it's no one's business but his own."

"I suppose not," Harry began. He pulled up shortly as the Hermit, followed by Jim, emerged from the tent.

The Hermit had a queer smile in his eyes, but Jim looked desperately uncomfortable.

Jim favoured the others with a heavy scowl as he came out of the tent, slipping behind the Hermit in order that he might deliver it unobserved. It was plain enough to fill them with considerable discomfort. They exchanged glances of bewilderment.

"I wonder what's up now?" Wally whispered.

Jim strolled over to them as the Hermit, without saying anything, crossed to his fireplace, and began to put some sticks together.

"You're bright objects!" he whispered wrathfully. "Why can't you speak softly if you must go gabbling about other people?"

"You don't mean to say he heard us?" Harry said, colouring.

"I do, then! We could hear every word you said, and it was jolly awkward for me. I didn't know which way to look."

"Was he wild?" whispered Wally.

"Blessed if I know. He just laughed in a queer way, until Norah stuck up for him, and then he looked grave. 'I'm lucky to have one friend,' he said, and walked out of the tent. You're a set of goats!" finished Jim comprehensively.

"Well, I'm not ashamed of what I said, anyhow!" Norah answered indignantly. She elevated her tip-tilted nose, and walked away to where the

Hermit was gathering sticks, into which occupation she promptly entered. The boys looked at each other.

"Well, I am — rather," Harry said. He disappeared into the scrub, returning presently with a log of wood as heavy as he could drag. Wally, seeing his idea, speedily followed suit, and Jim, after a stare, copied their example. They worked so hard that by the time the Hermit and Norah had the fire alight, quite a respectable stack of wood greeted the eye of the master of the camp. He looked genuinely pleased.

"Well, you are kind chaps," he said. "That will save me wood-carting for many a day, and it is a job that bothers my old back."

"We're very glad to get it for you, sir," Jim blurted, a trifle shamefacedly. A twinkle came into the Hermit's eyes as he looked at him.

"That's all square, Jim," he said quietly, and without any more being said the boys felt relieved. Evidently this Hermit was not a man to bear malice, even if he did overhear talk that wasn't meant for him.

"Well," said the Hermit, breaking a somewhat awkward silence, "it's about time we heard the dusky Billy, isn't it?"

"Quite time, I reckon," Jim replied. "Lazy young beggar!"

"Well, the billy's not boiling yet, although it's not far off it."

"There he is," Norah said quickly, as a long shout sounded near at hand. The Hermit quickly went off in its direction, and presently returned, followed by Billy, whose eyes were round as he glanced about the strange place in which he found himself, although otherwise no sign of surprise appeared on his sable countenance. He carried the bags containing the picnic expedition's supply of food, which Norah promptly fell to unpacking. An ample supply remained from lunch, and when displayed to advantage on the short grass of the clearing the meal looked very tempting. The Hermit's eyes glistened as Norah unpacked a bag of apples and oranges as a finishing touch.

"Fruit!" he said. "Oh, you lucky people! I wish there were fruit shops in the scrub. I can dispense with all the others, but one does miss fruit."

"Well, I'm glad we brought such a bagful, because I'm sure we don't want it," Norah said. "You must let us leave it with you, Mr. Hermit."

"Water's plenty boilin'," said Billy.

Tea was quickly brewed, and presently they were seated on the ground and making a hearty meal, as if the lunch of a few hours ago had never been.

"If a fellow can't get hungry in the bush," said Wally, holding out his hand for his fifth scone, "then he doesn't deserve ever to get hungry at all!" To which Jim replied, "Don't worry, old man — that's a fate that's never likely to overtake you!" Wally, whose hunger was of a generally prevailing kind, which usually afflicted him most in school hours, subsided meekly into his tea-cup.

They did not hurry over the meal, for everyone was a little lazy after the long day, and there was plenty of time to get home — the long summer evening was before them, and it would merge into the beauty of a moonlit night. So they "loafed" and chatted aimlessly, and drank huge quantities of the billy-tea, that is quite the nicest tea in the world, especially when it is stirred with a stick. And when they were really ashamed to eat any more they lay about on the grass, yarning, telling bush tales many and strange, and listening while the Hermit spun them old-world stories that made the time slip away wonderfully. It was with a sigh that Jim roused himself at last.

"Well," he said, "it's awfully nice being here, and I'm not in a bit of a hurry to go — are you, chaps?"

The chaps chorused "No."

"All the same, it's getting late," Jim went on, pulling out his watch, "later than I thought, my word! Come on — we'll have to hurry. Billy, you slip along and saddle up the ponies one-time quick!"

Billy departed noiselessly.

"He never said 'Plenty!' " said Wally disappointedly, gathering himself up from the grass.

"It was an oversight," Jim laughed. "Now then, Norah, come along. What about the miserable remains?"

"The remains aren't so miserable," said Norah, who was on her knees gathering up the fragments of the feast. "See, there's a lot of bread yet, ever so many scones, heaps of cake, and the fruit, to say nothing of butter and jam." She looked up shyly at the Hermit. "Would you — would you mind having them?"

The Hermit laughed.

"Not a bit!" he said. "I'm not proud, and it is really a treat to see civilised food again. I'll willingly act as your scavenger, Miss Norah."

Together they packed up the remnants, and the Hermit deposited them inside his tent. He rummaged for a minute in a bag near his bed, and presently came out with something in his hand.

"I amuse myself in my many odd moments by this sort of thing," he said. "Will you have it, Miss Norah?"

He put a photograph frame into her hand — a dainty thing, made from the native woods, cunningly jointed together and beautifully carved. Norah accepted it with pleasure.

"It's not anything," the Hermit disclaimed, "very rough, I'm afraid. But you can't do very good work when your pocket-knife is your only tool. I hope you'll forgive its shortcomings, Miss Norah, and keep it to remember the old hermit."

"I think it's lovely," Norah said, looking up with shining eyes, "and I'm ever so much obliged. I'll always keep it."

"Don't forget," the Hermit said, looking down at the flushed face. "And some day, perhaps, you'll all come again."

"We must hurry," Jim said.

They were all back at the lunching-place, and the sight of the sun, sinking far across the plain, recalled Jim to a sense of half-forgotten responsibility.

"It's every man for his own steed," he said. "Can you manage your old crock, Norah?"

"Don't you wish yours was half as good?" queried Norah, as she took the halter off Bobs and slipped the bit into his mouth.

Jim grinned.

"Knew I'd got her on a soft spot!" he murmured, wrestling with a refractory crupper.

Harry and Wally were already at their ponies. Billy, having fixed the load to his satisfaction on the pack mare, was standing on one foot on a log jutting over the creek, drawing the fish from their cool resting-place in the water. The bag came up, heavy and dripping — so heavy, indeed, that it proved the last straw for Billy's balance, and, after a wild struggle to remain on the log, he was forced to step off with great decision into the water, a movement accompanied with a decisive "Bust!" amidst wild mirth on the part of the boys. Luckily, the water was not knee deep, Billy regained the log, not much the worse, except in temper.

"Damp in there, Billy?" queried Wally, with a grave face.

"Plenty!" growled Billy, marching off the log with offended dignity and a dripping leg.

The Hermit had taken Norah's saddle and placed it on Bobs, girthing it up with the quick movements of a practised hand. Norah watched him keenly, and satisfaction crept into her eyes as, the job done, the old man stroked the pony's glossy neck, and Bobs, scenting a friend, put his nose into his hand.

"He likes you," Norah said. "He doesn't do that to everyone. Do you like horses?"

"Better than men," said the Hermit. "You've a good pony, Miss Norah."

"Yes, he's a beauty," the little girl said. "I've had him since he was a foal."

"He'll carry you home well. Fifteen miles, is it?"

"About that, I think."

"And we'll find Dad hanging over the home paddock gate, wondering where we are," said Jim, coming up, leading his pony. "We'll have to say goodnight, sir."

"Goodnight, and goodbye," said the Hermit, holding out his hand. "I'm sorry you've all got to go. Perhaps some other holidays —?"

"We'll come out," nodded Jim. He shook hands warmly. "And if ever you find your way in as far as our place —"

"I'm afraid not," said the Hermit hastily. "As I was explaining to Miss Norah, I'm a solitary animal. But I hope to see you all again."

The boys said "goodbye" and mounted. The Hermit held Bobs while Norah swung herself up — the pony was impatient to be gone.

"Goodbye," he said.

Norah looked at him pitifully.

"I won't say goodbye," she said. "I'm coming back — some day. So it's —'so long!' "

"So long," the old man echoed, rather drearily, holding her hand. Then something queer came into his eyes, for suddenly Norah bent from the saddle and kissed his cheek.

He stood long, watching the ponies and the lithe young figures scurrying across the plain. When they vanished he turned wearily and, with slow steps, went back into the scrub.

They forded the creek carefully, for the water was high, and it was dark in the shadows of the trees on the banks. Jim knew the way well, and so did Norah, and they led, followed by the other boys. When they had crossed, it was necessary to go steadily in the dim light. The track was only wide enough for them to ride in Indian file, which is not a method of locomotion which assists conversation, and they rode almost in silence.

It was queer, down there in the bush, with only the cries of far-off birds to break the quiet. Owls and mopokes hooted dismally, and once a great flapping thing flew into Harry's face, and he uttered a startled yell before he realised that it was only one of the night birds — whereat mirth ensued at the expense of Harry. Then to scare away the hooters they put silence to flight with choruses, and the old bush echoed to " 'Way Down Upon the Swanee River" and more modern songs, which aren't half as sweet as the old Christy Minstrel ditties. After they had exhausted all the choruses they knew, Harry "obliged" with one of Gordon's poems, recited with such boyish simplicity combined with vigour that it quite brought down the audience, who applauded so loudly that the orator was thankful for the darkness to conceal his blushes.

"Old Harry's our champion elocutioner at school, you know," Wally said. "You should have heard him last Speech Day! He got more clapping than all the rest put together."

"Shut up, young Wally!" growled Harry in tones of affected wrath.

"Same to you," said Wally cheerfully. "Why, you had all the mammas howling into their hankies in your encore piece!"

After which nothing would satisfy Norah but another recitation, and another after that; and then the timber ended, and there was only the level plain between them and home, with the moon just high enough to make it sufficiently light for a gallop. They tore wildly homeward, and landed in a slightly dishevelled bunch at the gate of the paddock.

No one was about the stables.

"Men all gone off somewhere," said Jim laconically, proceeding to let his pony go. His example was followed by each of the others, the steeds dismissed with a rub and a pat, and the saddles placed on the stands.

"Well, I don't know about you chaps," said Jim, "but I'm as hungry as a hunter!"

"Same here," chorused the chaps.

"Come along and see what good old Brownie's put by for us," said Norah, disappearing towards the house like a small comet.

The boys raced after her. In the kitchen doorway Mrs. Brown stood, her broad face resplendent with smiles.

"I was just beginning to wonder if any of you had fallen into the creek," she said. "You must be hungry, poor dears. Supper's ready."

"Where's Dad?" asked Norah.

"Your pa's gone to Sydney."

"Sydney!"

"Yes, my dears. A tallygrum came for him — something about some valuable cattle to be sold, as he wants."

"Oh," said Jim, "those shorthorns he was talking about?"

"Very like, Master Jim. Very sorry, your Pa were, he said, to go so suddint, and not to see you again, and the other young gentlemen likewise, seein' you go away on Monday. He left his love to Miss Norah, and a letter for you; and Miss Norah, you was to try not to be dull, and he would be back by Thursday, so he 'oped."

"Oh," said Norah, blankly. "It's hardly a home-coming without Dad."

Supper was over at last, and it had been a monumental meal. To behold the onslaughts made by the four upon Mrs. Brown's extensive preparations one might have supposed that they had previously been starving for time uncounted.

"Heigho!" said Jim. "Our last day tomorrow."

Groans followed from Harry and Wally.

"What do you want to remind a fellow for?"

"Couldn't help it — slipped out. What a jolly sell not to see old Dad again!" Jim wrinkled his brown handsome face into a frown.

"You needn't talk!" said Norah gloomily. "Fancy me on Monday — not a soul to speak to."

"Poor old Norah — yes, it's rough on you," said Jim. "Wish you were coming too. Why can't you get Dad to let you go to school in Melbourne?"

"Thanks," said Norah hastily, "I'd rather not. I think I can bear this better. School! What on earth would I do with myself, shut up all day?"

"Oh, all right; I thought you might like it. You get used to it, you know."

"I couldn't get used to doing without Dad," returned Norah.

"Or Dad to doing without you, I reckon," said Jim. "Oh, I suppose it's better as it is — only you'll have to get taught some day, old chap, I suppose."

"Oh, never mind that now," Norah said impatiently. "I suppose I'll have a governess some

day, and she won't let me ride astride, or go after
the cattle, or climb trees, or do anything worth
doing, and everything will be perfectly hateful. It's
simply beastly to be getting old!"

"Cheer up, old party," Jim laughed. "She might
be quite a decent sort for all you know. As for
riding astride, Dad'll never let you ride any other
way, so you can keep your mind easy about that.
Well, never mind governesses, anyhow; you
haven't got one yet, and sufficient unto the day is
the governess thereof. What are we going to do
tomorrow?"

"Can't do very much," said Norah, still showing
traces of gloom. "It's Sunday; besides, the horses
want a spell, and you boys will have to pack —
you leave pretty early on Monday, you know."

"Oh, botheration!" said Wally, jumping up so
suddenly that he upset his chair. "For goodness'
sake, don't talk of going back until we actually get
there; it's bad enough then. Let's go and explore
somewhere tomorrow."

"We can do that all right," said Jim, glad of any
turn being given to the melancholy conversation.
"We've never taken you chaps to the falls, two
miles up the creek, and they're worth seeing."

"It's a nice walk, too," added Norah, putting
sorrow to flight by deftly landing a pellet of bread
on Harry's nose. "Think you can struggle so far,
Harry?"

"Yes, and carry you back when you knock up,"
said that gentleman, returning the missile,
without success, Norah having retreated behind a
vase of roses. "I think it would be a jolly good
plan."

"Right oh!" said Jim. "That's settled. We'll pack up in the morning, get Brownie to give us dinner early, and start in good time. It doesn't really take long to walk there, you know, only we want to be able to loaf on the way, and when we get to the falls."

"Rather," said Harry. "I never see any fun in a walk when you tear somewhere, get there, and tear back again. Life's too short. Come on, Norah, and play to us."

So they trooped into the drawing-room, and for an hour the boys lay about on sofas and easy chairs, while Norah played softly. Finally she found that her entire audience was sound asleep, a state of things she very naturally resented by gently pouring water from a vase on their peaceful faces. Peace fled at that, and so did Norah.

CHAPTER 10

The Last Day

"NOW then, Harry, are you ready?"
"Coming," said Harry's cheerful voice. He appeared on the verandah, endeavouring to cram a gigantic apple into his pocket.

"Norah's," he said, in response to Jim's lifted eyebrows. "Don't know if she means to eat it in sections or not — it certainly doesn't mean to go into my pocket as it is." He desisted from his efforts. "Try it in the crown of your hat, old man."

"Thanks — my hat's got all it knows to hold my brains," retorted Jim. "You can't take that thing. Here, Norah," as that damsel appeared on the step, "how do you imagine Harry's going to cart this apple?"

"Quite simple," said Norah airily. "Cut it in four, and we'll each take a bit."

"That's the wisdom of Solomon," said Wally, who was lying full length on the lawn — recovering, as Jim unkindly suggested, from dinner.

"Well, come along," Jim said impatiently. "You're an awfully hard crowd to get started. We want to reach the falls in fair time, to see the sunlight on them — it's awfully pretty. After about three or four o'clock the trees shade the water, and it's quite ordinary."

"Just plain, wet water," murmured Wally. Jim rolled him over and over down the sloping lawn, and then fled, pursued by Wally with dishevelled attire and much grass in his mouth. The others followed more steadily, and all four struck across the paddock to the creek.

It was a rather hot afternoon, and they were glad to reach the shade of the bank and to follow the cattle track that led close to the water. Great fat bullocks lay about under the huge gum trees, scarcely raising their eyes to glance at the children as they passed; none were eating, all were chewing the cud in lazy contentment. They passed through a smaller paddock where superb sheep dotted the grass — real aristocrats these, accustomed to be handled and petted, and to live on the fat of the land — poor grass or rough country food they had never known. Jim and Norah visited some special favourites, and patted them. Harry and Wally admired at a distance.

"Those some of the sheep you saved from the fire?" queried Harry.

Norah flushed.

"Never did," she said shortly, and untruthfully. "Don't know why you can't talk sense, Jim!" — at which that maligned youth laughed excessively, until first the other boys, and then Norah, joined in, perforce.

After again climbing over the sheep-proof fence of the smaller paddock they came out upon a wide plain, almost treeless, save for the timber along the creek, where their cattle track still led them. Far as they could see no fence broke the line of yellow grass. There were groups of cattle out on the plain. These were store bullocks, Jim explained, a draft recently arrived from Queensland, and hardly yet acclimatised.

"It takes a good while for them to settle down," Norah said, "and then lots of 'em get sick — pleuro and things; and we inoculate them, and their tails drop off, and sometimes the sick ones get bad-tempered, and it's quite exciting work mustering."

"Dangerous?" asked Wally.

"Not with a pony that knows things like Bobs," said Bobs' mistress. "He always keeps his weather eye open for danger."

"Not a bad thing, as you certainly don't," laughed Jim.

"Well — do you?"

"Certainly I do," said Jim firmly, whereat Norah laughed very heartily.

"When I leave school, Dad says I can go on the roads with the cattle for one trip," said Jim. "Be no end of fun — takes ever so long to bring them down from Queensland, and the men have a real good time — travel with a cook, and a covered buggy and pair to bring the tucker and tents along."

"What'll you be?" asked Wally. "Cook?"

"No, slushy," said Harry.

"No, I'll take you two chaps along in those billets," grinned Jim.

"I don't know who'd be cook," said Norah solemnly: "but I don't think the men would be in very good condition at the end of the trip, whichever of you it was!"

With such pleasantries they beguiled the way,

until, on rounding a bend in the track, a dull roar came plainly to their ears.

"What's that?" asked Wally, stopping to listen.

"That's the falls, my boy," replied Jim. "They're really quite respectable falls — almost Niagarous! Come along, we'll see them in a couple of minutes."

The sound of falling water became plainer and plainer as they pushed on. At this point the track was less defined and the scrub thicker — Jim explained that the cattle did not come here much, as there was no drinking-place for them for a good distance below the falls. They might almost have imagined themselves back in the bush near the Hermit's camp, Harry said, as they pushed their way through scrub and undergrowth, many raspberry vines adding variety, if not charm, to the scramble. The last part of the walk was up hill, and at length they came out upon a clearer patch of ground.

For some time the noise of the falls had deepened, until now it was a loud roar; but the sound had hardly prepared the boys for the sight that met their gaze. High up were rocky cliffs, sparsely clothed with vegetation, and through these the creek had cut its way, falling in one sheer mass, fifty feet or more, into the bed below, hollowed out by it during countless ages. The water curved over the top of the fall in one exquisite wave, smooth as polished marble, but halfway down a point of rock jutted suddenly out, and on this the waters dashed and split, flying off from it in a cloud of spray. At the foot the cataract roared and bubbled and seethed in one boiling mass of rapids.

But the glory of it all was the sunlight. It fell right on the mass of descending water; and in the rays the fall glittered and flashed with all the colours of the rainbow, and the flying spray was like powdered jewels. It caught the drops hanging on the ferns that fringed the water, and turned them into twinkling diamonds. The whole fall seemed to be alive in the sunbeams' dancing light.

"Oh-h, I say," whispered Harry. "Fancy never showing us this before!" He cast himself on the ground and lay, chin in hands, gazing at the wonder before him.

"We kept it to the last," said Norah softly. She sat down by him and the others followed their example.

"Just think," said Harry, "that old creek's been doing that ever since time began — every day the sun comes to take his share at lighting it up, long before we were born, and ages after we shall die! Doesn't it make you feel small!"

Norah nodded understandingly. "I saw it once by moonlight," she said. "Dad and I rode here one night — full moon. Oh, it was lovely! Not like this, of course, because there wasn't any colour — but a beautiful white, clean light, and the fall was like a sheet of silver."

"Did you ever throw anything over?" asked Wally. His wonderment was subsiding and the boy in him woke up again.

"No good," said Jim. "You never see it again. I've thrown a stick in up above, and it simply whisks over and gets sucked underneath the curtain of water at once, and disappears altogether until it reaches the smooth water, ever so far down."

"Say you went over yourself?"

"Wouldn't be much left of you," Jim answered with a laugh. "The bed of the creek's simply full of rocks — you can see a spike sticking up here and there in the rapids. We've seen sheep come down in flood-time — they get battered to bits. I don't think I'll try any experiments, thank you, young Wally."

"You always were a disobliging critter," Wally grinned.

"Another time a canoe came over," Jim said. "It belonged to two chaps farther up — they'd just built it, and were out for the first time, and got down too near the falls. They didn't know much about managing their craft, and when the suck of the water began to take them along they couldn't get out of the current. They went faster and faster, struggling to paddle against the stream, instead of getting out at an angle and making for the bank — which they might have done. At last they could hear the roar of the falls quite plainly."

"What happened to them?" asked Wally. "Did they do over?"

"Well, they reckoned it wasn't healthy to remain in the canoe," said Jim. "It was simply spinning along in the current, and the falls were almost in sight. So they dived in, on opposite sides — the blessed canoe nearly tipped over when they stood up, and only the shock of the cross drive kept her right. Of course the creek's not so very wide, even farther up beyond the falls, and the force of their spring sent them nearly out of the current. They could both swim well, and after a struggle they got to the banks, just in time to see the canoe whisk over the waterfall!"

"What hard luck!"

"It was rather. They started off downstream to find it, but for a long way they couldn't see a trace. Then, right in the calm water, ever so far down, they found it — bit by bit. It was broken into so much matchwood!"

"What did they do?" asked Wally.

"Stood and stared at it from opposite sides, like two wet images," said Jim, laughing. "It's low-down to grin, I suppose, but they must have looked funny. Then one of them swam across and they made their way to our place, and we fixed them up with dry things and drove them home. I don't think they've gone in for canoeing since!" finished Jim reflectively.

"Well, I guess it would discourage them a bit," Wally agreed. "Getting shipwrecked's no fun."

"Ever tried it?"

"Once — in Albert Park Lagoon," Wally admitted bashfully. "Some of us went out for a sail one Saturday afternoon. We didn't know much about it, and I really don't know what it was that tipped the old boat over. I was the smallest, so naturally I wasn't having any say in managing her."

"That accounts for it," said Jim drily.

"Didn't mean that — goat!" said Wally. "Anyhow, I was very much astonished to find myself suddenly kicking in the mud. Ever been in that lake? It isn't nice. It isn't deep enough to drown you, but the mud is a caution. I got it all over me — face and all!"

"You must have looked your best!" said Jim.

"I did. I managed to stand up, very much amazed to find I wasn't drowned. Two of the others walked out! I was too small to do more than just manage to keep upright. The water was round my chest. I couldn't have walked a yard."

"How did you manage?"

"A boat came along and picked up the survivors," grinned Wally. "They wouldn't take us in. We were just caked with mud, so I don't blame 'em — but we hung on to the stern, and they towed us to the shore. We were quite close to land. Then they went back and brought our boat to us. They were jolly kind chaps — didn't seem to mind any trouble."

"You don't seem to have minded it, either," said Norah.

"We were too busy laughing," Wally said. "You have to expect these things when you go in for a life on the ocean wave. The worst part of it came afterwards, when we went home. That was really unpleasant. I was staying at my aunt's in Toorak."

"Did you get in a row?"

"It was unpleasant," Wally repeated. "Aunts haven't much sympathy, you know. They don't like mess, and I was no end messy. We won't talk about it, I think, thank you." Wally rolled over on his back, produced an apple and bit into it solemnly.

"Let us respect his silence," said Jim.

"You had aunts too?" queried Wally, with his mouth full.

"Not exactly aunts," Jim said. "But we had an old Tartar of a housekeeper once, when we were small kids. She ruled us with a rod of iron for about six months, and Norah and I could hardly call our souls our own. Father used to be a good deal away and Mrs. Lister could do pretty well as she liked."

"I did abominate that woman," said Norah reflectively.

"I don't wonder," replied Jim. "You certainly were a downtrodden little nipper as ever was. D'you remember the time we went canoeing in the flood on your old p'rambulator?"

"Not likely to forget it."

"What was it?" Wally asked. "Tell us, Jim."

"Norah had a pram — like most kids," Jim began.

"Well, I like that," said Norah, in great indignation. "It was yours first!"

"Never said it wasn't," said Jim, somewhat abashed by the laughter that ensued. "But that was ages ago. It was yours at this time, anyhow. But only the lower storey was left — just the floor of the pram on three wheels. Norah used to sit on this thing and push herself along with two sticks, like rowing on dry land."

"It was no end of fun," said Norah. "You *could* go!"

"You could," grinned Jim. "I'll never forget the day I saw you start from the top of the hill near the house. The pram got a rate on of a mile a minute, and the sticks weren't needed. About half-way down it struck a root, and turned three double somersaults in the air. I don't know how many Norah turned — but when Dad and I got to the spot she was sitting on a thick mat of grass, laughing like one o'clock, and the pram was about half a mile away on the flat with its wheels in the air! We quite reckoned you were killed."

"Yes, and Dad made me promise not to go down that hill again," said Norah ruefully. "It was a horrid nuisance!"

"Well, there was a flood," said Jim. "Not very much of a one. We'd had a good bit of rain, and the water-hole in the home paddock overflowed and covered all the flat about two feet deep. At first it was a bit too deep for Norah and her wheeled boat, but when it went down a bit she set off voyaging. She did look a rum little figure, out in the middle of the water, pushing herself along with her two sticks! Mrs. Lister didn't approve of it, but as Dad had given her leave, the housekeeper couldn't stop her."

At this point Norah was heard to murmur "Cat!"

"Just so!" said Jim. "Well, you know, I used to poke fun at Norah and this thing. But one day I had gone down to the water's edge, and she came up on it, poling herself through the water at a great rate, and it occurred to me it didn't look half bad fun. So I suggested a turn myself."

"You said, 'Here, kid, let's have that thing for a bit,' " said Norah firmly.

"Did I?" said Jim, with meekness.

"Yes, you did. So I kindly got off."

"Then?" asked Harry.

"He got on. I said, 'Jim, dear, pray be careful about the holes, and let me tell you where they are!' "

"I'm sure you did!" grinned Wally.

"And he said, 'If a kid like you can keep out of holes, I guess I can!' "

"I'm sure he did!" said Wally.

"Yes. So he set off. Now I had been over that flat so often in dry weather that I knew every bit of it. But Jim didn't. He went off as hard as he could, and got on very well for a little bit — "

"Am I telling this yarn, or are you?" inquired Jim, laughing.

"This is the part that is best for me to tell," said Norah solemnly. "Then he turned suddenly, so suddenly I hadn't time to do more than yell a warning, which he didn't hear — and the next minute the side wheels of the pram went over the edge of a hole, and the thing turned upside down upon poor old Jimmy!"

"How lovely!" said Wally, kicking with delight. "Well, and what happened?"

"Oh, Jim can tell you now," laughed Norah. "I wasn't under the water!"

"I was!" said Jim. "The blessed old pram turned clean over and cast me bodily into a hole. That was all I knew — until I tried to get out, and found the pram had come, too, and was right on top of me — and do you think I could move that blessed thing?"

"Well?"

"In came Norah," said Jim. "(I'll take it out of you now, my girl!) She realized at once what had happened and waded in from the bank and pulled the old pram off her poor little brother! I came up, spluttering, to see Norah, looking very white, just preparing to dive in after me!"

"You never saw such a drowned rat!" said Norah, taking up the tale. "Soaked — and muddy — and very cross! And the first thing he did was to abuse my poor old wheely-boat!"

"Well — wouldn't you?" Jim laughed. "Had to abuse something! Anyhow, we righted her and Norah waded farther in after the sticks, which had floated peacefully away, and we pulled the wheely-boat ashore. Then we roared laughing at each other. I certainly was a drowned rat, but Norah wasn't much better, as she'd slipped nearly into the hole herself, in pulling the pram off me. But when we'd laughed, the first thought was — 'How are we going to dodge Mrs. Lister?' It was a nasty problem!"

"What did you do?"

"Well, after consultation we got up near the house, planting the pram in some trees. We dodged through the shrubbery until we reached that old summer-house, and there I left Norah and scooted over to the stables, and borrowed an overcoat belonging to a boy we had working and a pair of his boots. Dad was away, or I might have gone straight to him. I put on the borrowed things over my wet togs (and very nice I looked!) and trotted off to the side of the house. No one seemed about, so I slipped into my room through the window and then into Norah's, and got a bundle of clothes, and back I scooted to the summer-house, left Norah's things there, and found a dressing-room for myself among some shrubs close by.

"Well, do you know, that old cat, Mrs. Lister, had seen us all the time? She'd actually spotted us coming up the paddock, dripping, and had deliberately planted herself to see what we'd do. She knew all about my expedition after clothes; then she followed us to the shrubbery, and descended upon us like an avalanche, just as we got half dressed!"

"'May I ask what you naughty little children are doing?' she said.

"Well, you know, that put my back up a bit — 'cause I was nearly twelve, and Dad didn't make a little kid of me. However, I tried to keep civil, and tell her what had happened; but she told me to hold my tongue. She grabbed Norah by the shoulder, and called her all the names under the sun, and shook her. Then she said, 'You'll come to bed at once, miss!' and caught hold of her wrist to drag her in.

"Now Norah had sprained her wrist not long before, and she had to be a bit careful of it. We all knew that. She didn't cry out when Mrs. Lister jerked her wrist, but I saw her turn white, and knew it was the bad one."

"So he chucked himself on top of old Mrs. Lister, and pounded her as hard as he could," put in Norah, "and she was so astonished she let me go. She turned her attention to Jim then, and gave him a terrible whack over the head that sent him flying. And just then we heard a voice that was so angry we hardly recognized it for Dad's, saying — 'What is this all about?' "

"My word, we were glad to see Dad!" said Jim. "He came over and put his arm round Norah — poor little kid. Mrs. Lister had screwed her wrist till it was worse than ever it had been, and she was as white as a sheet. Dad helped her on with her clothes. All the time Mrs. Lister was pouring out a flood of eloquence against us, and was nearly black in the face with rage. Dad took no notice until Norah was dressed. Then he said, 'Come to me in the study in twenty minutes,' and he picked Norah up and carried her inside, where he dosed her, and fixed up her wrist. I put on my clothes and followed them.

"Norah and I never said anything until Mrs. Lister had told her story, which was a fine production, little truth, and three parts awful crams. Then Dad asked for our side, and we just told him. He knew we never told lies, and he believed us, and we told him some other things Mrs. Lister used to do to us in the way of bullying and spite. I don't know that Dad needed them, because Norah's wrist spoke louder than fifty tales, and he didn't need any more evidence, though after all, she might have grabbed the bad wrist by mistake, and she had done far worse things on purpose. But the end of it was, Mrs. Lister departed that night, and Norah and I danced a polka in the hall when we heard the buggy drive off."

"That being the case," said Norah gravely, "we'll all have an apple."

The apples were produced and discussed, and then it was time to think of home, for the sun had long since left the glistening surface of the falls. So they gathered themselves up, and reluctantly enough left the beautiful scene behind them, with many a backward look.

The way home was rather silent. The shadow

of the boys' departure was over them all, and Norah especially felt the weight of approaching loneliness. With Dad at home it would have been easier to let the boys go, but the prospect of several days by herself, with only the servants for company, was not a very comforting one. Norah wished dismally that she had been born a boy, with the prospect of a journey, and mates, and school, and "no end of larks." Then she thought of Dad, and though still dismal, unwished the wish, and was content to remain a girl.

There was a little excitement on the homeward trip over a snake, which tried to slip away unseen through the grass, and when it found itself surrounded by enemies, coiled itself round Harry's leg, a proceeding very painful to that youth, who nevertheless stood like a statue while Jim dodged about for a chance to strike at the wildly waving head. He got it at last, and while the reptile writhed in very natural annoyance, Harry managed to get free, and soon put a respectful distance between himself and his too-affectionate acquaintance. Jim finished up the snake, and they resumed the track, keeping a careful look-out, and imagining another in every rustle.

"Well done, old Harry!" said Wally. "Stood like a statue, you did!"

"Thanks!" said Harry. "Jim's the chap to say 'Well done' to, I think."

"Not me," said Jim. "Easy enough to try to kill the brute. I'd rather do that than feel him round my leg, where I couldn't get at him."

"Well, I think I would, too," Harry said,

laughing. "I never felt such a desire to stampede in my life."

"It was beastly," affirmed Norah. She was a little pale. "It seemed about an hour before he poked his horrid old head out and let Jim get a whack at it. But you didn't lose much time then, Jimmy!"

"Could he have bitten through the leg of your pants?" queried Wally, with interest.

"He couldn't have sent all the venom through, I think," Jim replied. "But enough would have gone to make a very sick little Harry."

"It'd be an interesting experiment, no doubt," said Harry. "But, if you don't mind, I'll leave it for someone else to try. I'd recommend a wooden-legged man as the experimenter. He'd feel much more at his ease while the snake was trying how much venom he could get through a pant leg!"

CHAPTER 11

Goodbye

"I was just a-goin' to ring the big bell," said Mrs. Brown.

She was standing on the front verandah as the children came up the lawn.

"Why, we're not late, Brownie, are we?" asked Norah.

"Not very." The old housekeeper smiled at her. "Only when your Pa's away I allers feels a bit nervis about you — sech thoughtless young people, an' all them animals and snakes about!"

"Gammon!" said Jim, laughing. "D'you mean to say I can't look after them, Brownie?"

"I'd rather not say anythink rash, Master Jim," rejoined Mrs. Brown with a twinkle.

"I guess Mrs. Brown's got the measure of your foot, old man," grinned Harry.

"Oh, well," said Jim resignedly, "a chap never gets his due in this world. I forgive you, Brownie, though you don't deserve it. Got a nice tea for us?"

"Sech as it is, Master Jim, it's waitin' on you," said Mrs. Brown, with point.

"That's what you might call a broad hint," cried Jim. "Come on, chaps — race you for a wash-up!"

They scattered, Mrs. Brown laying violent hands on the indignant Norah, and insisting on

arraying her in a clean frock, which the victim
resisted, as totally unnecessary. Mrs. Brown made
her point, however, and a trim little maiden joined
the boys in the dining-room five minutes later.

Mrs. Brown's cooking was notable, and she had
excelled herself over the boys' farewell tea. A big
cold turkey sat side by side with a ham of majestic
dimensions, while the cool green of a salad was
tempting after the hot walk. There were jellies,
and a big bowl of fruit salad, while the centre of
the table was occupied by a tall cake, raising aloft
glittering white tiers. There were scones and tarts
and wee cakes, and dishes of fresh fruit, and
altogether the boys whistled long and softly, and
declared that "Brownie was no end of a brick!"

Whereat Mrs. Brown, hovering about to see that
her charges wanted nothing, smiled and blushed,
and said, "Get on, now, do!"

Jim carved, and Jim's carving was something to
marvel at. No method came amiss to him. When
he could cut straight he did: at other times he
sawed; and, when it seemed necessary, he dug.
After he had finished helping every one, Wally
said that the turkey looked as if a dog had been
at it, and the ham was worse, which remarks Jim
meekly accepted as his due. Nor did the inartistic
appearance of the turkey prevent the critic from
coming back for more!

Everyone was hungry, and did full justice to
"Brownie's" forethought; while Norah, behind the
tall teapot, declared that it was a job for two men
and a boy to pour out for such a thirsty trio. Harry
helped the fruit salad, and Harry's helpings were
based on his own hunger, and would have suited

Goliath. Finally, Norah cut the cake with great ceremony, and Wally's proposal that everyone should retire to the lawn with a "chunk" was carried unanimously.

Out on the grass they lay and chattered, while the dusk came down, and slowly a pale moon climbed up into the sky. Norah alone was silent. After a while Harry and Wally declared they must go and pack, and Jim and his sister were left alone.

Wally and Harry scurried down the hall. The sound of their merry voices died away, and there was silence on the lawn.

Jim rolled nearer to Norah.

"Blue, old girl?"

"'M," said a muffled voice.

Jim felt for her hand in the darkness — and found it. The small, brown fingers closed tightly round his rough paw.

"I know," he said comprehendingly. "I'm awfully sorry, old woman. I do wish we hadn't to go."

There was no answer. Jim knew why — and also knowing perfectly well that tears would mean the deepest shame, he talked on without requiring any response.

"Beastly hard luck," he said. "We don't want to go a bit — fancy school after this! Ugh! But there are three of us, so it isn't so bad. It wouldn't matter if Dad was at home, for you. But I must say it's low-down to be leaving you all by your lonely little self."

Norah struggled hard with that abominable lump in her throat, despising herself heartily.

"Brownie'll be awfully good to you," went on

Jim. "You'll have to buck up, you know, old girl, and not let yourself get dull. You practise like one o'clock; or make jam, or something; or get Brownie to let you do some cooking. Anything to keep you 'from broodin' on bein' a dorg,' as old David Harum says. There's all the pets to look after, you know — you've got to keep Billy up to the mark, or he'll never feed 'em properly, and if you let him alone he changes the water in the dishes when the last lot's dry. And, by George, Norah" — Jim had a bright idea — "Dad told me last night he meant to shift those new bullocks into the Long Plain. Ten to one he forgot all about it, going away so suddenly. You'll have to see to it."

"I'd like that," said Norah, feeling doubtfully for her voice.

"Rather — best thing you can do," Jim said eagerly. "Take Billy with you, of course, and a dog. They're not wild, and I don't think you'll have any trouble — only be very careful to get 'em all — examine all the scrub in the paddock. Billy knows how many there ought to be. I did know, but, of course, I've forgotten. Of course Dad may have left directions with one of the men about it already."

"Well, I could go too, couldn't I?" queried Norah.

"Rather. They'd be glad to have you."

"Well, I'll be glad of something to do. I wasn't looking forward to tomorrow."

"No," said Jim, "I know you weren't. Never mind, you keep busy. You might drive into Cunjee with Brownie on Tuesday — probably you'd get a letter from Dad a day earlier, and hear when he's coming home — and if he says he's coming on

Thursday, Wednesday won't seem a bit long. You'll be as right as ninepence if you buck up."

"I will, old chap. Only I wish you weren't going."

"So do I," said Jim, "and so do the other chaps. They want to come again some holidays."

"Well, I hope you'll bring them."

"My word! I will. Do you know, Norah, they think you're no end of a brick?"

"Do they?" said Norah, much pleased. "Did they tell you?"

"They're always telling me. Now, you go to bed, old girl."

He rose and pulled her to her feet.

Norah put up her arms round his neck — a very rare caress.

"Goodnight," she said. "I — I do love you, Jimmy!"

Jim hugged her.

"Same here, old chap," he said.

There was such scurrying in the early morning. Daylight revealed many things that had been overlooked in the packing overnight, and they had to be crammed in, somehow. Other things were remembered which had not been packed, and which must be found, and diligent hunt had to be made for them.

Norah was everybody's mate, running on several errands at once, finding Jim's school cap near Harry's overcoat while she was looking for Wally's cherished snake-skin. Her strong brown hands pulled tight the straps of bulging bags on which their perspiring owners knelt, puffing. After the said bags were closed and carried out to the buggy, she found the three toothbrushes, and crammed each, twisted in newspaper, into its owner's pocket. She had no time to think she was dull.

Mrs. Brown, who had been up since dawn, had packed a huge hamper, and superintended its placing in the buggy. It was addressed to "Master James, Master Harry and Master Wallie," and later Jim reported that its contents were such as to make the chaps at school speechless — a compliment which filled Mrs. Brown with dismay, and a wish that she had put in less pastry and perhaps a little castor oil. At present she felt mildly safe about it and watched it loaded with a sigh of relief.

"Boom-m-m!" went the big gong, and the boys rushed to the dining-room, where Norah was ready to pour out tea.

"You have some, Norah," said Harry, retaining his position close to the teapot, whence Wally had vainly striven to dislodge him.

"Yes, old girl, you eat some breakfast," commanded Jim.

Norah flashed a smile at him over the cosy.

"Lots of time afterwards," she said, a little sadly.

"No time like the present." Wally took a huge bite out of a scone, and surveyed the relic with interest. Someone put a smoking plateful before him, and his further utterances were lost in eggs and bacon.

Mrs. Brown flitted about like a stout guardian angel, keeping an especially watchful eye on Jim. If the supply on his plate lessened perceptibly, it was replenished with more, like manna from above. To his laughing protests she merely murmured, "Poor dear lamb!" whereat Wally and Harry laughed consumedly, and Jim blushed.

"Well, you've beaten me at last, Brownie," Jim declared finally. He waved away a chop which was about to descend upon his plate. "No, truly, Brownie dear; there are limits! Tea? No thanks, Norah, I've had about a dozen cups already, I believe! You fellows ready?"

They were, and the table was briskly deserted. There was a final survey of the boys' room, which resembled a rubbish heap, owing to vigorous packing. Everybody ran wildly about looking for something. Wally was found searching frantically for his cap, which Norah discovered — on his head. There was a hurried journey to the kitchen, to bid the servants "Goodbye."

The buggy wheels scrunched the gravel before the hall door. The overseer coo-ee'd softly.

"All aboard!"

"All right, Evans!" Jim appeared in the doorway, staggering under a big Gladstone bag. Billy, similarly laden, followed. His black face was unusually solemn.

"Chuck 'em in, Billy. Come on, you chaps!"

The chaps appeared.

"Goodbye, Norah. It's been grand!" Harry pumped her hand vigorously.

"Wish you were coming!" said Wally dismally. "Goodbye. Write to us, won't you, Norah?"

"Now then, Master Jim!" Evans glanced at his watch.

"Right oh!" said Jim. He put his arm round the little girl's shoulders and looked keenly into her face. There was no hint of breaking down. Norah met his gaze steadily and smiled at him. But the boy knew.

"Goodbye, little chap," he said, and kissed her. "You'll keep your pecker up?"

She nodded. "Goodbye, Jimmy, old boy."

Jim sprang into the buggy.

"All right, Evans."

They whirled down the drive. Looking back, waving their caps, the boys carried away a memory of a brave little figure, erect, smiling and lonely on the doorstep.

CHAPTER 12

The Winfield Murder

THE next few days went by slowly enough. Norah followed faithfully all Jim's plans for her amusement. She practised, did some cooking, and helped Mrs. Brown preserve apricots; then there were the pets to look to and, best of all, the bullocks to move from one paddock to another. It was an easy job, and Evans was quite willing to leave it to Norah, Billy and a dog. The trio made a great business of it, and managed almost to forget loneliness in the work of hunting through the scrub and chasing the big, sleepy half-fat beasts out upon the clear plain. There were supposed to be forty-four in the paddock, but Norah and Billy mustered forty-five, and were exceeding proud of themselves in consequence.

Next day Norah persuaded Mrs. Brown to allow herself to be driven into Cunjee. There was nothing particular to go for, except that, as Norah said, they would get the mail a day earlier; but Mrs. Brown was not likely to refuse anything that would chase the look of loneliness from her charge's face. Accordingly they set off after an

early lunch, Norah driving the pair of brown
ponies in a light single buggy that barely held her
and her by no means fairy-like companion.

The road was good and they made the distance
in excellent time, arriving in Cunjee to see the
daily train puff its way out of the station. Then
they separated, as Norah had no opinion whatever
of Mrs. Brown's shopping — principally in drapers'
establishments, which this bush maiden hated
cordially. So Mrs. Brown, unhampered, plunged
into mysteries of flannel and sheeting, while
Norah strolled up the principal street and exchanged greetings with those she knew.

She paused by the door of a blacksmith's shop,
for the smith and she were old friends, and Norah
regarded Blake as quite the principal person of
Cunjee. Generally there were horses to be looked
at, but just now the shop was empty, and Blake
came forward to talk to the girl.

"Seen the p'lice out your way?" he asked
presently, after the weather, the crops, and the
dullness of business had been exhausted as topics.

"Police?" queried Norah. "No. Why?"

"There was two mounted men rode out in your
direction yesterday," Blake answered. "They're on
the track of that Winfield murderer, they believe."

"What was that?" asked Norah blankly. "I never
heard of it."

"Not heard of the Winfield murder! Why, you
can't read the papers, missy, surely?"

"No; of course I don't," Norah said. "Daddy
doesn't like me to read the everyday ones."

Blake nodded.

"No, I s'pose not," he said. "You're too young to

worry your little head about murders and
such-like. But everybody was talkin' about the
Winfield affair, so I sorter took it for granted that
you'd know about it."

"Well, I don't," said Norah. "What is it all
about?"

"There's not very much I can tell you about it,
missy," Blake said, scratching his head and
looking down at the grave face. "Nobody knows
much about it.

"Winfield's a little bit of a place about twenty
miles from 'ere, you know — right in the bush and
away from any rail or coach line. On'y a couple o'
stores, an' a hotel, an' a few houses. Don't suppose
many people out o' this district ever heard of it,
it's that quiet an' asleep.

"Well, there was two ol' men livin' together in
a little hut a mile or so from the Winfield
township. Prospectors, they said they were — an'
there was an idea that they'd done pretty well at
the game, an' had a bit of gold hidden somewhere
about their camp. They kept very much to
themselves, an' never mixed with anyone — when
one o' them came into the township for stores he'd
get his business done an' clear out as quick as
possible.

"Well, about a month ago two fellows called
Bowen was riding along a bush track between
Winfield an' their camp when they came across
one o' the ol' mates peggin' along the track for all
he was worth. They was surprised to see that he
was carryin' a big swag, an' was apparently on a
move.

" 'Hullo, Harris!' they says — "leavin' the

district?' He was a civil spoken ol' chap as a rule, so they was rather surprised when he on'y give a sort o' grunt, an' hurried on.

"They was after cattle, and pretty late the same day they found themselves near the hut where the two ol' chaps lived, an', as they was hungry an' thirsty, they reckoned they'd call in an' see if they could get a feed. So they rode up and tied their horses to a tree and walked up to the hut. No one answered their knock, so they opened the door, an' walked in. There, lyin' on his bunk, was ol' Waters. They spoke to him, but he didn't answer. You see, missy, he couldn't, bein' dead."

"Dead!" said Norah, her eyes dilating.

Blake nodded.

"Stone dead," he said. "They thought at first he'd just died natural, as there was no mark o' violence on 'im, but when they got a doctor to examine 'im he soon found out very different. The poor ol' feller 'ad been poisoned, missy; the doctor said 'e must a' bin dead twelve hours when the Bowens found 'im. Everything of value was gone from the hut along with his mate, old Harris — the black-hearted villain he must be!"

"Why, do they think he killed the other man?" Norah asked.

"Seems pretty certain, missy," Blake replied. "In fact, there don't seem the shadder of a doubt. He was comin' straight from the hut when the Bowens met 'im — an' he'd cleared out the whole place, gold an' all. Oh, there ain't any doubt about Mr. Harris bein' the guilty party. The only thing doubtful is Mr. Harris' whereabouts."

"Have the police been looking for him?" asked Norah.

"Huntin' high an' low — without any luck. He seems to have vanished off the earth. They've bin follerin' up first one clue and then another without any result. Now the last is that he's been seen somewhere the other side of your place, an' two troopers have gone out today to see if there's any truth in the rumour."

"I think it's awfully exciting," Norah said, "but I'm terribly sorry for the poor man who was killed. What a wicked old wretch the other must be! — his own mate, too! I wonder what he was like. Did you know him?"

"Well, I've seen old Harris a few times — not often," Blake replied. "Still, he wasn't the sort of old man you'd forget. Not a bad-looking old chap, he was. Very tall and well set up, with piercin' blue eyes, long white hair an' beard, an' a pretty uppish way of talkin'. I don't fancy anyone about here knew him very well — he had a way of keepin' to himself. One thing, there's plenty lookin' out for him now."

"I suppose so," Norah said. "I wonder will he really get away?"

"Mighty small chance," said Blake. "Still, it's wonderful how he's managed to keep out of sight for so long. Of course, once in the bush it might be hard to find him — but sooner or later he must come out to some township for tucker, an' then everyone will be lookin' out for him. They may have got him up your way by now, missy. Is your Pa at home?"

"He's coming home in a day or two," Norah said,

"perhaps tomorrow. I hope they won't find Harris
and bring him to our place."

"Well, it all depends on where they find him if
they do get him," Blake replied. "Possibly they
might find the station a handy place to stop at.
However, missy, don't you worry your head about
it — nothing for you to be frightened about."

"Why, I'm not frightened," Norah said. "It hasn't
got anything to do with me. Only I don't want to
see a man who could kill his mate, that's all."

"He's much like any other man," said Blake
philosophically. "Say, here's someone comin' after
you, missy, I think."

"I thought I'd find you here," exclaimed Mrs.
Brown's fat, comfortable voice, as its owner puffed
her way up the slope leading to the blacksmith's.
"Good afternoon, Mr Blake. I've finished all my
shopping, Miss Norah, my dear, and the mail's in,
and here's a letter for you, as you won't be sorry
to see."

"From Dad? How lovely!" and Norah snatching
at the grey envelope with its big, black writing,
tore it open hastily. At the first few words, she
uttered a cry of delight.

"Oh, he's coming home tomorrow, Brownie —
only another day! He says he thinks it's time he
was home, with murderers roaming about the
district!" and Norah executed a few steps of a
Highland fling, greatly to the edification of the
blacksmith.

"Dear sakes alive!" said Mrs. Brown,
truculently. "I think there are enough of us at the
station to look after you, murderer or no murderer
— not as 'ow but that 'Arris must be a nasty

creature! Still I'm very glad your Pa's coming, Miss Norah, because nothing do seem right when he's away — an' it's dull for you, all alone."

"Master Jim gone back, I s'pose?" queried Blake.

"Yesterday," Norah added.

"Then you must be lonely," the old blacksmith said, taking Norah's small brown hand, and holding it for a moment in his horny fist very much as if he feared it were an eggshell, and not to be dropped. "Master Jim's growing a big fellow, too — goin' to be as big a man as his father, I believe. Well, goodbye, missy, and don't forget to come in next time you're in the township."

There was nothing further to detain them in Cunjee, and very soon the ponies were fetched from the stables, and they were bowling out along the smooth metal road that wound its way across the plain, and Norah was mingling excited little outbursts of delight over her father's return with frequent searches into a big bag of sweets which Mrs. Brown had thoughtfully placed on the seat of the buggy.

"I don't know why Blake wanted to go telling you about that nasty murderer," Mrs. Brown said. They were ten miles from Cunjee, and the metal road had given place to a bush track, in very fair order.

"Why not?" asked Norah, with the carelessness of twelve years.

"Well, tales of murders aren't the things for young ladies' ears," Mrs. Brown said primly. "Your Pa never tells you such things. The paper's been full of this murder, but I would 'a' scorned to talk to you about it."

"I don't think Blake meant any harm," said Norah. "He didn't say so very much. I don't suppose he'd have mentioned it, only that Mr. Harris is supposed to have come our way, and even that doesn't seem certain."

"'Arris 'as baffled the police," said Mrs. Brown, with the solemn pride felt by so many at the worsting of the guardians of the law. "They don't reely know anythink about his movements, that's my belief. Why, it's weeks since he was seen. This yarn about his comin' this way is on'y got up to 'ide the fact that they don't know a thing about it. I don't b'lieve he's anywhere within coo-ee of our place. Might be out of the country now, for all anyone's sure of."

"Blake seemed to think he'd really come this way," Norah said.

"Well, I'll keep a look-out for him, at any rate," laughed Norah. "He ought to be easy enough to find — tall and good-looking and well set up — whatever that may mean — and long white beard and hair. He must be a pretty striking-looking sort of old man. I — " And then recollection swept over Norah like a flood, and her words faltered on her lips.

Her hands gripped the reins tighter, and she drove on unconsciously. Blake's words were beating in her ears. "Not a bad-looking old chap — very tall and well set up — piercing blue eyes and a pretty uppish way of talking." The description had meant nothing to her until someone whom it fitted all too aptly had drifted across her mental vision.

The Hermit! Even while she felt and told herself

that it could not be, the fatal accuracy of the likeness made her shudder. It was perfect — the tall, white-haired old man — "not the sort of old man you'd forget" — with his distinguished look; the piercing blue eyes — but Norah knew what kindliness lay in their depths — the gentle refined voice, so different from most of the rough country voices. It would answer to Blake's "pretty uppish way of talking." Anyone who had read the description would, on meeting the Hermit, immediately identify him as the man for whom the police were searching. Norah's common sense told her that.

A wave of horror swept over the little girl, and the hands gripping the reins trembled. Common sense might tell one tale, but every instinct of her heart told a very different one. That gentle-faced old man, with a world of kindness in his tired eyes — he the man who killed his sleeping mate for a handful of gold! Norah set her square little chin. She would not — could not — believe it.

"Why, you're very quiet, dearie." Mrs. Brown glanced inquiringly at her companion. "A minute ago you was chatterin', and now you've gone down flat, like old soda-water. Is anything wrong?"

"No, I'm all right, Brownie. I was only thinking," said Norah, forcing a smile.

"Too many sweeties, I expect," said Mrs. Brown, laying a heavy hand on the bag and impounding it for future reference. "Mustn't have you get indigestion, an' your Pa comin' home tomorrow."

Norah laughed.

"Now, did you ever know me to have indigestion in my life?" she queried.

"Well, perhaps not," Mrs. Brown admitted. "Still, you never can tell; it don' do to pride oneself on anything. If it ain't indigestion, you've been thinking too much of this narsty murder."

Norah flicked the off pony deliberately with her whip.

"Darkie is getting disgracefully lazy," she said. "He's not doing a bit of the work. Blackie's worth two of him." The injured Darkie shot forward with a bound, and Mrs. Brown grabbed the side of the buggy hastily, and in her fears at the pace for the ensuing five minutes forgot her too inconvenient cross-examination.

Norah settled back into silence, her forehead puckered with a frown. She had never in her careless little life been confronted by such a problem as the one that now held her thoughts. That the startling similarity between her new-made friend and the description of the murderer should fasten upon her mind was unavoidable. She struggled against the idea as disloyal, but finally decided to think it out calmly.

The descriptions tallied. So much was certain. The verbal likeness of one man was an exact word painting of the other, so far as it went, "though," as poor Norah reflected, "you can't always tell a person just by hearing what he's like." Then there was no denying that the conduct of the Hermit would excite suspicion. He was camping alone in the deepest recesses of a lonely tract of scrub; he had been there some weeks, and she had had plenty of proof that he was taken aback at being discovered, and wished earnestly that no future prowlers might find their way to his retreat. She recalled his shrinking from the boys, and his hasty refusal to go to the homestead. He had said in so many words that he desired nothing so much as to be left alone — anyone would have gathered that he feared discovery. They had all been conscious of the mystery about him. Her thoughts flew back to the half-laughing conversation between Harry and Wally, when they had actually speculated as to why he was hiding. Putting the case fairly and squarely, Norah had to admit that it looked black against the Hermit.

Against it, what had she? No proof; only a remembrance of two honest eyes looking sadly at her; of a face that had irresistibly drawn her confidence and friendship; of a voice whose tones had seemed to echo sincerity and kindness. It was absolutely beyond Norah's power to believe that the hand that had held hers so gently could have been the one to strike to death an unsuspecting mate. Her whole nature revolted against the thought that her friend could be so base.

"He was in trouble," Norah said, over and over again, in her uneasy mind, "he was unhappy. But I know he wasn't wicked. Why, Bobs made friends with him!"

The thought put fresh confidence in her mind; Bobs always knew "a good sort."

"I won't say anything," she decided at last, as they wheeled round the corner of the homestead. "If they knew there was a tall old man there, they'd go and hunt him out, and annoy him horribly. I know he's all right. I'll hold my tongue about him altogether — even to Dad."

The coach dropped Mr. Linton the next day at

the Cross Roads, where a little figure, clad in white linen, sat in the buggy, holding the brown ponies, while the dusky Billy was an attendant sprite on his piebald mare.

"Well, my little girl, it's good to see you again," Mr. Linton said, putting his Gladstone bag into the buggy and receiving undismayed a small avalanche of little daughter upon his neck. "Steady, dear — mind the ponies." He jumped in, and put his arm round her. "Everything well?"

"Yes, all right, Daddy. I'm so glad to have you back!"

"Not gladder than I am to get back, my little lass," said her father. "Good day, Billy. Let 'em go, Norah."

"Did you see Jim?" asked Norah, as the ponies bounded forward.

"No — missed him. I had only an hour in town, and went out to the school, to find Master Jim had gone down the river — rowing practice. I was sorry to miss him; but it wasn't worth waiting another day in town."

"Jim would be sorry," said Norah thoughtfully. She herself was rather glad: had Jim seen his father most probably he would have mentioned the Hermit. Now she had only his letters to fear, and as Jim's letters were of the briefest nature and very far apart, it was not an acute danger.

"Yes, I suppose he would," Mr. Linton replied. "I regretted not having sent a telegram to say I was going to the school — it slipped my memory. I had rather a rush, you know. I suppose you've been pretty dull, my girlie?"

"Oh, it was horrid after the boys went," Norah

said. "I didn't know what to do with myself, and the house was terribly quiet. It was hard luck that you had to go away, too."

"Yes, I was very sorry it happened so," her father said. "Had we been alone together I'd have taken you with me, but we'll have the trip some other time. Did you have a good day's fishing on Saturday?"

"Yes," said Norah, flushing a little guiltily — the natural impulse to tell all about their friend the Hermit was so strong. "We had a lovely day, and caught ever so many fish — didn't get home till ever so late. The only bad part was finding you away when we got back."

"Well, I'm glad you had good luck, at any rate," Mr. Linton said. "So Anglers' Bend is keeping up its reputation, eh? We'll have to go out there, I think, Norah; what do you say about it? Would you and Billy like a three days' jaunt on fishing bent?"

"Oh, it would be glorious, Daddy! Camping out?"

"Well, of course — since we'd be away three days. In this weather it would be a very good thing to do, I think."

"You are a blessed Daddy," declared his daughter, rubbing her cheek against his shoulder. "I never knew anyone with such beautiful ideas." She jigged on her seat with delight. "Oh, and, Daddy, I'll be able to put you on to such a splendid new hole for fishing!"

"Will you, indeed?" said Mr. Linton, smiling at the flushed face. "That's good, dear. But how did you discover it?"

Norah's face fell suddenly. She hesitated and looked uncomfortable.

"Oh," she said slowly, "I — we — found it out last trip."

"Well, we'll go, Norah — as soon as I can fix it up," said her father. "And now, have you heard anything about the Winfield murderer?"

"Not a thing, Daddy. Brownie thinks it's just a yarn that he was seen about here."

"Oh, I don't think so at all," Mr. Linton said. "A good many people have the idea, at any rate — of course they may be wrong. I'm afraid Brownie is rather too ready to form wild opinions on some matters. To tell the truth, I was rather worried at the reports — I don't fancy the notion of escaped gentry of that kind wandering round in the vicinity of my small daughter."

"Well, I don't think you need have worried," said Norah, laughing up at him, "but all the same, I'm not a bit sorry you did, if it brought you home a day earlier, Dad!"

"Well, it certainly did," said Mr. Linton, pulling her ear, "but I'm not sorry either. I can't stand more than a day or two in town. As for the murderer, I'm not going to waste any thought on him now that I am here. There's the gate, and here comes Billy like a whirlwind to open it."

They bowled through the gate and up the long drive, under the arching boughs of the big gum trees, that formed a natural avenue on each side. At the garden gate Mrs. Brown stood waiting, with a broad smile of welcome, and a chorus of barks testified to the arrival of sundry dogs. "It's a real home-coming," Mr. Linton said as he walked up the path, his hand on Norah's shoulder — and the little girl's answering smile needed no words. They turned the corner by the big rose bush, and came within view of the house, and suddenly Norah's smile faded. A trooper in dusty uniform stood on the doorstep.

"Why, that's a pleasant object to greet a man," Mr. Linton said, as the policeman turned and came to meet him with a civil salute. He nodded as the man came up. "Did you want me?"

"It's only about there 'ere murderer, sir," said the trooper. "Some of us is on a sort of a scent, but we haven't got fairly on to his tracks yet. I've ridden from Mulgoa today, and I came to ask if your people had seen anything of such a chap passing — as a swaggie or anything?"

"Not that I know of," said Mr. Linton. "What is he like?"

"Big fellow — old — plenty of white hair and beard, though, of course, they're probably cut off by this time. Very decent-looking chap," said the trooper reflectively, "an' a good way of speakin'."

"Well, I've seen no such man," said Mr. Linton decidedly. "Of course, though, I don't see all the 'travellers' who call. Perhaps Mrs. Brown can help you."

"Not me, sir," said Mrs. Brown, with firmness. "There ain't been no such a person — and you may be sure there ain't none I don't see! Fact is, when I saw as 'ow the murderer was supposed to be in this districk, I made inquiries amongst the men and none of them had seen any such man as the papers described. I reckon 'e may just as well be

in any other districk as this — I s'pose the poor
p'lice must say 'e's somewheres!"

She glared defiantly at the downcast trooper.

"Wish you had the job of findin' him, mum," said
that individual. "Well, sir, there's no one else I
could make inquiries of, is there?"

"Mrs. Brown seems to have gone the rounds,"
Mr. Linton said. "I really don't think there's
anyone else — unless my small daughter here can
help you," he added laughingly.

But Norah had slipped away, foreseeing possible
questioning.

The trooper smiled.

"Don't think I need worry such a small witness,"
he said. "No, I'll just move on, Mr. Linton. I'm
beginning to think I'm on a wild-goose chase."

CHAPTER 13

The Circus

THE days went by, but no further word of the Winfield murderer came to the anxious ears of the little girl at Billabong homestead. Norah never read the papers, and could not therefore satisfy her mind by their reports; but all her inquiries were met by the same reply, "Nothing fresh." The police were still in the district — so much she knew, for she had caught glimpses of them when out riding with her father. The stern-looking men in dusty uniforms were unusual figures in those quiet parts. But Norah could not manage to discover if they had searched the scrub that hid the Hermit's simple camp; and the mystery of the Winfield murder seemed as far from being cleared up as ever.

Meanwhile there was plenty to distract her mind from such disquieting matters. The station work happened to be particularly engrossing just then, and day after day saw Norah in the saddle, close to her father's big black mare, riding over hills and plains, bringing up the slow sheep or galloping gloriously after cattle that declined to be mustered. There were visits of inspection to be made to the farthest portions of the run, and busy days in the yards, when the men worked at drafting the stock, and Norah sat perched on the high "cap" of a fence and, watching with all her eager little soul in her eyes, wished heartily that she had been born a boy. Then there were a couple of trips with Mr. Linton to outlying townships, and on one of these occasions Norah had a piece of marvellous luck, for there was actually a circus in Cunjee — a real, magnificent circus, with lions and tigers and hyenas, and a camel, and other beautiful animals, and, best of all, a splendid elephant of meek and mild demeanour. It was the elephant that broke up Norah's calmness.

"Oh, Daddy!" she said. "Daddy! Oh, can't we stay?"

Mr. Linton laughed.

"I was expecting that," he said. "Stay? And what would Brownie be thinking?"

Norah's face fell.

"Oh," she said. "I'd forgotten Brownie. I s'pose it wouldn't do. But isn't it a glorious elephant, Daddy?"

"It is, indeed," said Mr. Linton, laughing. "I think it's too glorious to leave, girlie. Fact is, I had an inkling the circus was to be here, so I told Brownie not to expect us until she saw us. She put a basket in the buggy, with your toothbrush, I think."

The face of his small daughter was sufficient reward.

"Daddy!" she said. "Oh, but you are the MOST Daddy!" Words failed her at that point.

Norah said that it was a most wonderful "spree." They had dinner at the hotel, where the waiter called her "Miss Linton," and in all ways behaved precisely as if she were grown up, and after dinner she and her father sat on the balcony while Mr. Linton smoked and Norah watched the population arriving to attend the circus. They came from all quarters — comfortable old farm wagons, containing whole families; a few smart buggies; but the majority came on horseback, old as well as young. The girls rode in their dresses, or else had slipped on habit skirts over their gayer attire, with great indifference as to whether it happened to be crushed, and they had huge hats, trimmed with all the colours of the rainbow. Norah did not know much about dress, but it seemed to her theirs was queer. But one and all looked so happy and excited that dress was the last thing that mattered.

It seemed to Norah a long while before Mr. Linton shook the ashes from his pipe deliberately and pulled out his watch. She was inwardly dancing with impatience.

"Half-past seven," remarked her father, shutting up his watch with a click. "Well, I suppose we'd better go, Norah. All ready, dear?"

"Yes, Daddy. Must I wear gloves?"

"Why, not that I know of," said her father, looking puzzled. "Hardly necessary, I think. I don't wear 'em. Do you want to?"

"Goodness — no!" said his daughter hastily.

"Well, that's all right," said Mr. Linton. "Stow them in my pocket and come along."

Out in the street there were unusual signs of bustle. People were hurrying along the footpath. The blare of brass instruments came from the big circus tent, round which was lingering every small boy of Cunjee who could not gain admission. Horses were tied to adjoining fences, considerably disquieted by the brazen strains of the band. It was very cheerful and inspiring, and Norah capered gently as she trotted along by her father.

Mr. Linton gave up his tickets at the first tent, and they passed in to view the menagerie — a queer collection, but wonderful enough in the eyes of Cunjee. The big elephant held pride of place, as he stood in his corner and sleepily waved his trunk at the aggravating flies. Norah loved him from the first, and in a moment was stroking his trunk, somewhat to her father's anxiety.

"I hope he's safe?" he asked an attendant.

"Bless you, yes, sir," said that worthy, resplendent in dingy scarlet uniform. "He alwuz knows if people ain't afraid of him. Try him with this, missy." "This" was an apple, and Jumbo deigned to accept it at Norah's hands, and crunched it serenely.

"He's just dear," said Norah, parting reluctantly from the huge swaying brute and giving him a final pat as she went.

"Better than Bobs?" asked her father.

"Pooh!" said Norah loftily. "What's this rum thing?"

"A wildebeest," read her father. "He doesn't look like it."

"Pretty tame beast, I think," Norah observed, surveying the stolid-looking animal before her. "Show me something really wild, Daddy."

"How about this chap?" asked Mr. Linton.

They were before the tiger's cage, and the big yellow brute was walking up and down with long stealthy strides, his great eyes roving over the curious faces in front of him. Someone poked a stick at him — an attention which met an instant roar and spring on the tiger's part, and a quick, and stinging rebuke from an attendant, before which the poker of the stick fled precipitately. The crowd, which had jumped back as one man, pressed nearer to the cage, and the tiger resumed his quick, silent prowl. But his eyes no longer roved over the faces. They remained fixed upon the man who had provoked him.

"How do you like him?" Mr. Linton asked his daughter.

Norah hesitated.

"He's not nice, of course," she said. "But I'm so awfully sorry for him, aren't you, Daddy? It does seem horrible — a great, splendid thing like that shut up for always in that little box of a cage. You feel he really ought to have a great stretch of jungle to roam in."

"And eat men in? I think he's better where he is."

"Well, you'd think the world was big enough for him to have a place apart from men altogether," said Norah, holding to her point sturdily. "Somewhere that isn't much wanted — a sandy desert, or a spare Alp! This doesn't seem right, somehow. I think I've seen enough animals, Daddy, and it's smelly here. Let's go into the circus."

The circus tent was fairly crowded as Norah and her father made their way in and took the seats reserved for them, under the direction of another official in dingy scarlet. Round the ring the tiers of seats rose abruptly, each tier a mass of eager, interested faces. A lame seller of fruit and drinks hobbled about crying his wares; at intervals came the "pop" of a lemonade bottle, and there was a steady crunching of peanut shells. The scent of orange peel rose over the circus smell — that weird compound of animal and sawdust and acetylene lamps. In the midst of all was the ring, with its surface banked up towards the outer edge.

They had hardly taken their seats when the band suddenly struck up in its perch near the entrance, and the company entered to the inspiring strains. First came the elephant, very lazy and stately — gorgeously caparisoned now, with a gaily attired "mahout" upon his neck. Behind him came the camel; and then the cages with the other occupants of the menagerie, looking either bored or fierce. They circled round the ring and then filed out.

The band struck up a fresh strain and in cantered a lovely lady on a chestnut horse. She wore a scarlet hat and habit, and looked to Norah very like a Christmas card. Round the ring she dashed gaily, and behind her came another lady equally beautiful in a green habit, on a black horse; and a third, wearing a habit of pale blue plush, who managed a piebald horse. Then came some girls in bright frocks, on beautiful ponies; and some boys, in tights, on other ponies; and then men, also in tights of every colour in the rainbow, who rode round with bored expressions, as if it were really too slow a thing merely to sit on a horse's back, instead of pirouetting there upon one foot. They flashed round once or twice and were gone, and Norah sat back and gasped, feeling that she had had a glimpse into another world — as indeed she had.

A little figure whirled into the ring — a tiny girl on a jet-black pony. She was sitting sideways at first, but as the pony settled into its stride round the ring she suddenly leaped to her feet and, standing poised, kissed her hands gaily to the audience. Then she capered first on one foot, then on another; she sat down, facing the tail, and lay flat along the pony's back; she assumed every position except the natural one. She leapt to the ground (to Norah's intense horror, who imagined she didn't mean to), and, running fiercely at the pony, sprang on his back again, while he galloped the harder. Lastly, she dropped a handkerchief, which she easily recovered by the simple expedient of hanging head downwards, suspended by one foot, and then galloped out of the ring, amid the frantic applause of Cunjee.

"Could you do that, Norah?" laughed Mr. Linton.

"Me?" said Norah amazedly, "me? Oh, fancy me ever thinking I could ride a bit!"

One of the lovely ladies, in a glistening suit of black, covered with spangles, next entered. She also preferred to ride standing, but was by no means idle. A gentleman in the ring obligingly handed her up many necessaries — plates and saucers and knives — and she threw these about the air, as she galloped, with great apparent carelessness, yet never failed to catch each just as it seemed certain to fall. Tiring of this pursuit, she flung them all back at the gentleman with deadly aim, while he, resenting nothing, caught them cleverly, and disposed of them to a clown who stood by, open-mouthed. Then the gentleman hung bright ribbons across the ring, apparently with the unpleasant intention of sweeping the lady from her horse — an intention which she frustrated by lightly leaping over each in turn, while her horse galloped beneath it. Finally, the gentleman — whose ideas really seemed most unfriendly — suddenly confronted her with a great paper-covered hoop, the very sight of which would have made an ordinary horse shy wildly — but even at this obstacle the lady did not lose courage. Instead, she leaped straight through the hoop, paper and all, and was carried out by her faithful steed, amidst yells of applause.

Norah gasped.

"Oh, isn't it perfectly lovely, Daddy!" she said.

Perhaps you boys and girls who live in cities, or near townships where travelling companies pay yearly visits, can have no idea of what this first circus meant to this little bush maid, who had lived all her twelve years without seeing anything half so wonderful. Perhaps, too, you are lucky to have so many chances of seeing things — but it is something to possess nowadays, even at twelve, the unspoiled, fresh mind that Norah brought to her first circus.

Everything was absolutely real to her. The clown was a being almost too good for this world, seeing that his whole time was spent in making people laugh uproariously, and that he was so wonderfully unselfish in the way he allowed himself to be kicked and knocked about — always landing in positions so excruciatingly droll that you quite forgot to ask if he were hurt. All the ladies who galloped round the ring, and did such marvellous things, treating a mettled steed as though he were as motionless as a kitchen table, seemed to Norah models of beauty and grace. There was one who set her heart beating by her daring, for she not only leaped through a paper-covered hoop, but through three, one after the other, and then — marvel of marvels — through one on which the paper was alight and blazing fiercely! Norah held her breath, expecting to see her scorched and smouldering at the very least; but the heroic rider galloped on, without seeming so much as singed. Almost as wonderful was the total indifference of the horses to the strange sights around them.

"Bobs would be off his head!" said Norah.

She was especially enchanted with a small boy and girl who rode in on the same pony, and had all sorts of capers, as much off the pony's back as upon it. Not that it troubled them to be off, because they simply ran, together, at the pony, and landed simultaneously, standing on his back, while the gallant steed galloped the more furiously. They hung head downwards while the pony jumped over hurdles, to their great apparent danger; they even wrestled, standing, and the girl pitched the boy off to the accompaniment of loud strains from the band and wild cheers from Cunjee. Not that the boy minded — he picked himself up and raced the pony desperately round the ring — the girl standing and shrieking encouragement, the pony racing, the boy scudding in front, until he suddenly turned and bolted out of the ring, the pony following at his heels, but never quite catching him — so that the boy really won, after all, which Norah thought was quite as it should be.

Then there were the acrobats — accomplished men in tight clothes — who cut the most amazing somersaults, and seemed to regard no object as too great to be leaped over. They brought in the horses, and stood ever so many of them together, backed up by the elephant, and the leading acrobat jumped over them all without any apparent effort. After which all the horses galloped off of their own accord, and "put themselves away" without giving anyone any trouble. Then the acrobats were hauled up into the top of the tent, where they swung themselves from rope to rope, and somersaulted through space; and one man hung head downwards, and caught by the hands another who came flying through the air as if he belonged there. Once he missed the outstretched hands, and Norah gasped, expecting to see him terribly hurt — instead of which he fell harmlessly into a big net thoughtfully spread for his reception, and rebounded like a tennis ball, kissing his hand gracefully to the audience; after which he again whirled through the air, and this time landed safely in the hands of the hanging man, who had all this while seemed just as comfortable head downwards as any other way. There was even a little boy who swung himself about the tent as fearlessly as the grown men, and cut capers almost as dangerous as theirs. Norah couldn't help

breathing more freely when the acrobats bowed
their final farewell.

Mr. Linton consulted his programme.

"They're bringing in the lion next," he said.

The band struck up the liveliest of tunes. All
the ring was clear now, except for the clown, who
suddenly assumed an appearance of great
solemnity. He marched to the edge of the ring and
struck an attitude indicative of profound respect.

In came the elephant, lightly harnessed, and
drawing a huge cage on wheels. On both sides
marched attendants in special uniforms, and on
the elephant's back stood the lion tamer, all
glorious in scarlet and gold, so that he was almost
hurtful to the eye. In the cage three lions paced
ceaselessly up and down. The band blared. The
people clapped. The clown bowed his forehead into
the dust and said feelingly, "Wow!"

Beside the ring was another, more like a huge
iron safe than a ring, as it was completely walled
and roofed with iron bars. The cage was drawn up
close beside this, and the doors slid back. The lions
needed no further invitation. They gave smothered
growls as they leaped from their close quarters
into this larger breathing space. Then another
door was opened stealthily, and the lion tamer
slipped in, armed with no weapon more deadly
than a heavy whip.

Norah did not like it. It seemed to her, to put
it mildly, a risky proceeding. Generally speaking,
Norah was by no means a careful soul, and had
no opinion of people who thought over much about
looking after their skins; but this business of lions
was not exactly what she had been used to. They

appeared to her so hungry, and so remarkably ill-tempered; and the man was as one to three, and had, apparently, no advantage in the matter of teeth and claws.

"Don't like this game," said the bush maiden, frowning. "Is he safe, Daddy?"

"Oh, he's all right," her father answered, smiling. "These chaps know how to take care of themselves, and the lions know he's master. Watch them, Norah."

Norah was already doing that. The lions prowling around the ring, keeping wary eyes on their tamer, were called to duty by a sharp crack of the whip. Growling, they took their respective stations — two on the seats of chairs, the third standing between them, poised on the two chair backs. Then they were put through a quick succession of tricks. They jumped over chairs and ropes and each other; they raced round the ring, taking hurdles at intervals; they balanced on big wooden balls, and pushed them along by quick changes of position. Then they leaped through hoops, ornamented with fluttering strips of paper, and clearly did not care for the exercise. And all the while their stealthy eyes never left those of the tamer.

"How do you like it?" asked Mr. Linton.

"It's beastly!" said Norah, with surprising suddenness. "I hate it, Daddy. Such big, beautiful things, and to make them do silly tricks like these; just as you'd train a kitten!"

"Well, they're nothing more than big cats," laughed her father.

"I don't care. It's — it's mean, I think. I don't

wonder they're cross. And you can see they are, Daddy. If I was a lion I know I'd want to bite somebody!"

The lions certainly did seem cross. They growled constantly, and were slow to obey orders. The whip was always cracking, and once or twice a big lioness, who was especially sulky, received a sharp cut. The outside attendants kept close to the cage, armed with long iron bars. Norah thought, watching them, that they were somewhat uneasy. For herself, she knew she would be very glad when the lion "turn" was over.

The smaller tricks were finished, and the tamer made ready for the grand "chariot act." He dragged forward an iron chariot and to it harnessed the smaller lions with stout straps, coupling the reins to a hook on the front of the little vehicle. Then he signalled to the lioness to take her place as driver.

The lioness did not move. She crouched down, watching him with hungry, savage eyes. The trainer took a step forward, raising his whip.

"You — Queen!" he said sharply.

She growled, not stirring. A sudden movement of the lions behind him made the trainer glance round quickly.

There was a roar, and a yellow streak cleft the air. A child's voice screamed. The tamer's spring aside was too late. He went down on his face, the lioness upon him.

Norah's cry rang out over the circus, just as the lioness sprang — too late for the trainer, however. The girl was on her feet, clutching her father.

"Oh, Daddy — Daddy!" she said.

All was wildest confusion. Men were shouting, women screaming — two girls fainted, slipping down, motionless, unnoticed heaps, from their seats. Circus men yelled contradictory orders. Within the ring the lioness crouched over the fallen man, her angry eyes roving about the disordered tent.

The two lions in the chariot were making furious attempts to break away. Luckily their harness was strong, and they were so close to the edge of the ring that the attendants were able, with their iron bars, to keep them in check. After a few blows they settled down, growling, but subdued.

But to rescue the trainer was not so easy a matter. He lay in the very centre of the ring, beyond the reach of any weapons; and not a man would venture within the great cage. The attendants shouted at the lioness, brandished irons, cracked whips. She heard them unmoved. Once she shifted her position slightly and a moan came from the man underneath.

"This is awful," Mr. Linton said. He left his seat in the front row and went across the ring to the group of white-faced men. "Can't you shoot the brute?" he asked.

"We'd do it in a minute," the proprietor answered. "But who'd shoot and take the chance of hitting Joe? Look at the way they are — it's ten to one he'd get hit." He shook his head. "Well, I guess it's up to me to go in and tackle her — I'd get a better shot inside the ring." He moved forward.

A white-faced woman flung herself upon him

and clung to him desperately. Norah hardly recognised her as the gay lady who had so merrily jumped through the burning hoops a little while ago. "You shan't go, Dave!" she cried, sobbing. "You mustn't! Think of the kiddies! Joe hasn't got a wife and little uns."

The circus proprietor tried to loosen her hold.

"I've got to, my girl," he said gently. "I can't leave a man o' mine to that brute. It's my fault — I orter known better than to let him take her from them cubs tonight. Let go, dear." He tried to unclinch her hands from his coat.

"Has she — the lioness — got little cubs?"

It was Norah's voice, and Mr. Linton started to find her at his side. Norah, very pale and shaky, with wide eyes, glowing with a great idea.

The circus man nodded. "Two."

"Wouldn't she — " Norah's voice was trembling almost beyond the power of speech — "wouldn't she go to them if you showed them to her — put them in the small cage? My — my old cat would!"

"By the powers!" said the proprietor. "Fetch 'em, Dick — run." The clown ran, his grotesque draperies contrasting oddly enough with his errand.

In an instant he was back, two fluffy yellow heaps in his arms. One whined as they drew near the cage, and the lioness looked up sharply with a growl. The clown held the cubs in her view, and she growled again, evidently uneasy. Beneath her the man was quiet now.

"The cage — quick!"

The big lion cage, its open door communicating with the ring, stood ready. The clown opened another door and slipped in the protesting cubs.

They made for the further door, but were checked
by the stout cords fastened to their collars. He held
them in leash, in full view of the lioness. She
growled and moved, but did not leave her prey.

"Make 'em sing out!" the woman said sharply.

Someone handed the clown an iron rod
sharpened at one end. He passed it through the
bars, and prodded a cub on the foot. It whined
angrily, and a quick growl came from the ring.

"Harder, Dick!"

The clown obeyed. There was a sharp, amazed
yelp of pain from the cub, and an answering roar
from the mother. Another protesting cry — and
then again that yellow streak as the lioness left
her prey and sprang to her baby, with a deafening
roar. The clown tugged the cubs sharply back into
the recesses of the cage as the mother hurled
herself through the narrow opening. Behind her
the bars rattled into place and she was restored
to captivity.

It was the work of only a moment to rush into
the ring, where the tamer lay huddled and
motionless. Kind hands lifted him and carried him
away beyond the performance tent, with its eager
spectators. The attendants quickly unharnessed
the two tame lions, and they were removed in
another cage, brought in by the elephant for their
benefit.

Norah slipped a hot, trembling hand into her
father's.

"Let's go, Daddy — I've had enough."

"More than enough, I think," said Mr. Linton.
"Come on, little girl."

They slipped out in the wake of the anxious

procession that carried the tamer. As they went, a performing goat and monkey passed them on their way to the ring, and the clown capered behind them. They heard his cheerful shout, "Here we are again!" and the laughter of the crowd as the show was resumed.

"Plucky chap, that clown," Mr. Linton said.

In the fresh air the men had laid the tamer down gently, and a doctor was bending over him, examining him by the flickering light of torches held by hands that found it hard to be steady.

"Not so much damaged as he might be," the doctor announced, rising. "That shoulder will take a bit of healing, but he looks healthy. His padded uniform has saved his life. Let's get him to the private hospital up the street. Everything necessary is there, and I'd like to have his shoulder dressed before he regains consciousness."

The men lifted the improvised stretcher again, and passed on with it. Norah and her father were following, when a voice called them. The wife of the circus proprietor ran after them — a strange figure enough, in her scarlet riding dress, the paint on her face streaked with tear marks.

"I'd like to know who you are," she said, catching Norah's hand. "But for you my man 'ud 'a been in the ring with that brute. None of us had the sense to think o' bringin' in the cubs. Tell me your name, dearie."

Norah told her unwillingly. "Nothing to make a fuss over," she added, in great confusion.

"I guess you saved Joe's life, an' perhaps my Dave's as well," the woman said. "We won't forget you. Goodnight, sir, an' thank you both."

Norah had no wish to be thanked, being of
opinion that she had done less than nothing at all.
She was feeling rather sick, and — amazing
feeling for Norah — inclined to cry. She was very
glad to get into bed at the hotel, and eagerly
welcomed her father's suggestion that he should
sit for a while in her room. Norah did not know
that it was dawn before Mr. Linton left his watch
by the restless sleeper, quiet now, and sought his
own couch.

She woke late, from a dream of lions and
elephants, and men who moaned softly. Her father
was by her bedside.

"Breakfast, lazy bones," he said.

"How's the tamer?" queried Norah, sitting up.

"Getting on all right. He wants to see you."

"Me!" said Norah. "Whatever for?"

"We've got to find that out," said her father,
withdrawing.

They found out after breakfast, when a grateful,
white-faced man, swathed in bandages,
stammered broken thanks.

"For it was you callin' out that saved me first,"
he said. "I'd never 'a thought to jump, but I heard
you sing out to me, an' if I hadn't she'd a broke
my neck, sure. An' then it was you thought o'
bringing in the cubs. Well, missy, I won't forget
you long's I live."

The nurse, at his nod, brought out the skin of
a young tiger, beautifully marked and made into
a rug.

"If you wouldn't mind takin' that from me,"
explained the tamer. "I'd like to feel you had it,
an' I'd like to shake hands with you, missy."

Outside the room Norah turned a flushed face to her father.

"Do let's go home, Daddy," she begged. "Cunjee's too embarrassing for me!"

CHAPTER 14

Camping Out

A BOUT that fishing excursion, Norah!"
"Yes, Daddy." A small brown paw slid itself
into Mr. Linton's hand.

They were sitting on the verandah in the
stillness of an autumn evening, watching the
shadows on the lawn become vague and indistinct,
and finally merge into one haze of dusk. Mr.
Linton had been silent for a long time. Norah
always knew when her father wanted to talk. This
evening she was content to be silent, too, leaning
against his knee in her own friendly fashion as
she curled up at his feet.

"Oh, you hadn't forgotten, then?"

"Well — not much! Only I didn't know if you
really wanted to go, Daddy."

"Why, yes," said her father. "I think it would be
rather a good idea, my girlie. There's not much
doing on the place just now. I could easily be
spared. And we don't want to leave our trip until
the days grow shorter. The moon will be right, too.
It will be full in four or five days — I forget the
exact date. So, altogether, Norah, I think we'd
better consult Brownie about the commissariat
department, and make our arrangements to go
immediately."

"It'll be simply lovely," said his daughter, breathing a long sigh of delight. "Such a long time since we had a camping out — just you and me, Daddy."

"Yes, it's a good while. Well, we've got to make up for lost time by catching plenty of fish," said Mr. Linton. "I hope you haven't forgotten the whereabouts of that fine new hole of yours? You'll have to take me to it if Anglers' Bend doesn't come up to expectations."

A deep flush came into Norah's face. For a little while she had almost forgotten the Hermit — or, rather, he had ceased to occupy a prominent position in her mind, since the talk of the Winfield murder had begun to die away. The troopers, unsuccessful in their quest, had gone back to headquarters, and Norah had breathed more freely, knowing that her friend had escaped — this time. Still, she never felt comfortable in her mind about him. Never before had she kept any secret from her father, and the fact of this concealment was apt to come home closely to her at times and cloud the perfect friendship between them.

"Master Billy will be delighted, I expect," went on Mr. Linton, not noticing the little girl's silence. "Anything out of the ordinary groove of civilization is a joy to that young man." He smiled. "He's the best hand with horses we ever had on the station. Now, Norah, come and talk to Brownie."

Mrs. Brown, on being consulted, saw no difficulties in the way. A day, she declared, was all she wanted to prepare sufficient food for the party for a week — let alone for only three days.

"Not as I'll stint you to three days," remarked

the prudent Brownie. "Last time it was to be three days — an' 'twas more like six when we saw you again. Once you two gets away — " and she wagged a stern forefinger at her employer. "And there's that black himp — he eats enough for five!"

"You forget the fish we're going to live on," laughed Mr. Linton.

"'M," said Brownie solemnly. "First catch your fish!"

"Why, of course, we mean to, you horrid old thing!" cried Norah laughing, "and bring you home loads, too — not that you deserve it for doubting us!"

"I have seen many fishing parties go out, Miss Norah, my dear," said Mrs. Brown impassively, "and on the 'ole more came 'ome hempty 'anded than bringing loads — fish bein' curious things, an' very unreliable on the bite. Still, we'll 'ope for the best — an' meanwhile to prepare for the worst. I'll just cook a few extry little things — another tongue, now, an' a nice piece of corned beef, an' per'aps a 'am. An' do you think you could manage a pie or two, Miss Norah?"

"Try her!" said Mr. Linton, laughing.

"Let's tell Billy!" — and off went Norah at a gallop.

She returned a few minutes later, slightly crestfallen.

"Billy must be asleep," she said. "I couldn't get an answer."

"Billy has no use for the day after the sun goes down, unless he's going possuming," her father said. "Never mind — the news will keep until the morning."

"Oh, I know," said Norah, smiling. "But I wanted to tell him tonight."

"I sympathise with you," said her father, "and, meanwhile, to console yourself, suppose you bend your mighty mind to the problem of getting away. Do you see any objection to our leaving for parts unknown the day after tomorrow?"

"Depends on Brownie and the tucker," said Norah practically.

"That part's all right, Brownie guarantees to have everything ready tomorrow night, if you help her."

"Why, of course I will, Daddy."

"And you have to get your own preparations made."

"That won't take long," said Norah, with a grin. "Brush, comb, toothbrush, pyjamas; that's all, Dad!"

"Such minor things as soap and towels don't appear to enter into your calculations," said her father. "Well, I can bear it!"

"Oh, you silly old Dad! Of course I know about those. Only Brownie always packs the ordinary, uninteresting things."

"I foresee a busy day for you and Brownie tomorrow," Mr. Linton said. "I'll have a laborious time myself, fixing up fishing tackle — if Jim and his merry men left me with any. As for Billy, he will spend the day grubbing for bait. Wherefore, everything being settled, come and play me, 'The Last Rose of Summer,' and then say goodnight."

Norah was up early, and the day passed swiftly in a whirl of preparations. Everything was ready by evening, including a hamper of monumental proportions, the consumption of which, Mr. Linton said, would certainly render the party unfit for active exertion in the way of fishing. Billy's delight had made itself manifest in the broad grin which he wore all day while he dug for worms, and chased crickets and grasshoppers. The horses were brought in and stabled overnight, so that an early start might be made.

It was quite an exciting day, and Norah was positive that she could not go to sleep when her father sent her off to bed at an unusually early hour, meeting her remonstrances with the reminder that she had to be up with, or before, the lark. However, she was really tired, and was soon asleep. It seemed to her that she had only been in this blissful condition for three minutes when a hand was laid on her shoulder and she started up to find daylight had come. Mr. Linton stood laughing at her sleepy face.

"D'you mean to say it's morning?" said Norah.

"I've been led to believe so," her father rejoined. "Shall I pull you out, or would you prefer to rise without assistance?"

"I'd much prefer to go to sleep again — but I'll tumble out, thank you," said his daughter, suiting the action to the word. "Had your bath, Daddy?"

"Just going to it."

"Then I'll race you!" said Norah, snatching a towel and disappearing down the hall, a slender, flying figure in blue pyjamas. Mr. Linton gave chase, but Norah's start was too good, and the click of the lock greeted him as he arrived at the door of the bathroom. The noise of the shower drowned his laughing threats, while a small voice sang, amid splashes, "You should have been here last week!"

Breakfast was a merry meal, although, as Norah said, it was unreasonable to expect anybody to have an appetite at that hour. Still, with a view to the future, and to avoid wounding Mrs. Brown too deeply, they made as firm an attempt as possible, with surprisingly good results. Then brief goodbyes were said, the pack scientifically adjusted to the saddle on the old mare, and they rode off in the cool, dewy morning.

This time there was no "racing and chasing o'er Cannobie Lea" on the way to Anglers' Bend. Mr. Linton's days of scurrying were over, he said, unless a bullock happened to have a difference of opinion as to the way he should go, and, as racing by one's self is a poor thing Norah was content to ride along steadily by her father's side, with only an occasional canter, when Bobs pulled and reefed as if he were as anxious to gallop as his young mistress could possibly be. It was time for lunch when they at length arrived at the well-remembered bend on the creek.

The horses were unsaddled and hobbled, and then turned out to wander at their own sweet will — the shortness of the hobbles a guarantee that they would not stray very far; and the three wanderers sat on the bank of the creek, very ready for the luncheon Mrs. Brown had carefully prepared and placed near the top of the pack. This despatched, preparations were made for pitching camp.

Here luck favoured them, for a visit to their former camping place showed that tent poles and pegs were still there, and uninjured — which considerably lessened the labour of pitching the tents. In a very short time the two tents were standing, and a couple of stretchers rigged up with bags — Mr. Linton had no opinion of the comfort of sleeping on beds of leaves. While her father and Billy were at this work, Norah unpacked the cooking utensils and provisions. Most of the latter were encased in calico bags, which could be hung in the shade, secure from either ants or flies, the remainder, packed in tins, being stowed away easily in the corner of one of the tents.

When the stretchers were ready Norah unpacked the bedding and made their beds. Finally she hung the toothbrushes to the ridge poles, and said contentedly, "Daddy, it's just like home!"

"Glad you think so!" said Mr. Linton, casting an approving eye over the comfortable-looking camp; and really there is something wonderfully home-like about a well-pitched camp with a few arrangements for comfort. "At any rate, I think we'll manage very well for a few days, Norah. Now, while Billy lays in a stock of firewood and fixes up a "humpy" for himself to sleep in, suppose you and I go down and try to catch some fish for tea?"

"Plenty," laughed Norah.

It soon became evident that Anglers' Bend was going to maintain its name as a place for fish. Scarcely was Norah's line in the water before a big black fish was on the hook, and after that the fun was fast and furious, until they had caught enough for two or three meals. The day was ideal for fishing — grey and warm, with just enough breeze to ripple the water faintly. Mr. Linton and Norah found it very peaceful, sitting together on the old log that jutted across the stream, and the time passed quickly. Billy at length appeared, and was given the fish to prepare, and then father and daughter returned to camp. Mr. Linton lit the fire, and cutting two stout forked stakes, which he drove into the ground, one on each side of the fire, he hung a green ti-tree pole across, in readiness to hold the billy and frying-pan. Billy presently came up with the fish, and soon a cheery sound of sizzling smote the evening air. By the time that Norah had "the table set," as she phrased it, the fish were ready, and in Norah's opinion no meal ever tasted half so good.

After it was over, Billy the indispensable removed the plates and washed up, and Norah and her father sat by the fire and "yarned" in the cool dusk. Not for long, for soon the little girl began to feel sleepy after the full day in the open air, and the prospect of the comfortable stretcher in her tent was very tempting. She brushed her hair outside in the moonlight, because a small tent is not the place in which to wield a hair-brush; then she slipped into bed, and her father came and tucked her up before tying the flap of her tent securely enough to keep out possible intruders in the shape of "bears" and possums. Norah lay watching the flickering firelight for a little while, thinking there was nothing so glorious as the open-air feeling, and the night scents of the bush; then she fell asleep.

"Ha-ha-ha-ha-ha! Ho-ho-ho-ho-ho!!"

A cheeky jackass on a gum tree bough fairly roared with laughter, and Norah woke up with a violent start. The sunlight was streaming across her bed. For a moment she was puzzled, wondering where she was; then the walls of the tent caught her eye, and she laughed at herself, and then lay still in the very pleasure of the dewy morning and the wonderful freshness of the air. For there is a delight in awaking after a night in the open that the finest house in the world cannot give.

Presently the flap of the tent was parted and Mr. Linton peeped in.

"Hallo!" he said, smiling, "did the old jackass wake you? I found him as good as an alarum clock myself. How about a swim?"

"Oh — rather!" said Norah, tumbling out of bed. She slipped on a jacket and shoes, and presently joined her father, and they threaded their way through the scrub until they came to a part of the creek where a beach, flat and sandy, and shelving down to a fairly deep hole, offered glorious bathing. Mr. Linton left Norah here, and himself went a few yards farther up, round a bend in the creek.

At the first plunge the water was distinctly cold, but once the first dip was taken Norah forgot all about chilliness, and only revelled in the delights of that big pool. She could swim like a fish — her father had seen to that in the big lagoon at home. Not until Mr. Linton's warning voice sang out that it was time to dress did she leave the water, and then with reluctance.

A brisk rub down with a hard towel and she rejoined her father. He cast an approving look at her glowing face.

"Well, you look as if you'd enjoyed your swim," he said.

"Oh, it was lovely, Daddy! Did you have a good bathe?"

"Yes — I struck a very good place — deep enough to dive in," her father answered. "Not that I counsel diving altogether — you strike such a lot of mud at the bottom — soft, sticky, black mud! I spent most of my bathe in getting myself clean after my dive! Still, I had a good swim, notwithstanding. I say, Norah, I'm ready for breakfast."

"So am I," said his daughter. "I hope Billy's got the fish on!"

However, there was no sign of him when they reached the camp. The fire was blazing and the billy boiling, but of the other Billy no trace existed.

"He's gone after the horses," Mr. Linton said. "I told him to see to them — but he ought to be back. I hope they're all right. Well, you get dressed, Norah."

By the time Norah's toilet was completed the fish, under Mr. Linton's supervision, were in the pan, and she hurried to set out the breakfast things. They were just beginning breakfast when the sound of hoofs was heard and Billy rode into the clearing on his own pony, with evident signs of perturbation on his face.

"What's up, Billy?" Mr. Linton asked sharply.

"That feller pack-mare," Billy said briefly. "Broken hobbles — clear out. Plenty!" He produced a hobble as he spoke, the broken leather telling its own tale.

Mr. Linton uttered an exclamation of anger.

"That comes of not seeing to the hobbles myself," he said sharply. "No sign of her?"

Billy shook his head.

"Not likely," Mr. Linton said. "That old mare would make for home like a shot. I daresay she's halfway there by now. Well, Billy, there's only one thing to do — get your pony saddled and go after her."

Billy's face expressed unuttered depths of woe.

"Get your breakfast first," said his master, "there's no particular hurry, for you're bound to have to go all the way home — and bring some good hobbles back with you, if you do!"

Billy slid to the ground.

"Plenty!" he said ruefully.

Billy, a vision of despondency, had faded away into the distance, making his chestnut pony pay for the disappointment of his long ride back the homestead for the missing mare. Norah and her father had "cleaned up house" as Norah put it, and again they were sitting on the old log that spanned the creek.

Their lines were in the water, but the fish were shy. The promise of a hot day had driven them to the shady hollows under the banks. The juiciest worms failed to lure them from their hiding-places. Norah thought it dull and said so.

Her father laughed.

"You'll never make a fisherman without cultivating an extra stock of patience," he said.

"The thought of last night's luck ought to make you happy."

"Well, it doesn't," his daughter answered decidedly. "That was yesterday, and this is today; and it is dull, Daddy, anyhow."

"Well, keep on hoping," said Mr. Linton. "Luck may change at any minute. Norah, do you know, I have something to tell you?"

"What?" Norah's dullness was gone. There was something unusual in her father's tone.

"I'm afraid you won't think it the best news," he said, smiling at her eager face. "But it had to come some day, I suppose. I couldn't keep you a baby always. There's a tutor coming to make a learned lady of my little bush maid."

"Daddy!" There were worlds of horror in the tone.

"Oh, don't!" said her father. "You make me feel a criminal of the deepest dye. What can I do with you, you ignorant small child? I can't let you grow up altogether a bush duffer, dear." His voice was almost apologetic. "I can assure you it might have been worse. Your Aunt Eva has been harrowing my very soul to make me send you to a boarding school. Think of that now!"

"Boarding school!" said Norah faintly. "Daddy, you wouldn't?"

"No — not at present, certainly," said her father. "But I had to agree to something — and, really, I knew it was time. You're twelve, you know, Norah. Be reasonable."

"Oh, all right," said Norah, swallowing her disgust. "If you say it's got to be, it has to be,

that's all, Daddy. My goodness, how I will hate it!
Have I got to learn heaps of things?"

"Loads," said her father, nodding. "Latin, and
French, and drawing, and geography, and how to
talk grammar, and any number of things I never
knew. Then you can teach the tutor things —
riding, and cooking, and knitting, and the care of
tame wallabies, and any number of things he
never dreamed of. He's a town young man, Norah,
and horribly ignorant of all useful arts."

"I'll turn him over to Billy after school," said
Norah laughing. "Is he nice, Dad?"

"Very, I should say," rejoined her father. "He's
the son of an old friend" — and his face saddened
imperceptibly. "Your Aunt Eva said it ought to be
a governess, and perhaps it would have been one
only young Stephenson came in my way. He
wanted something to do, and for his father's sake
I chose him for my daughter's instructor."

"Who's his father, Daddy?"

"Well, you wouldn't know if I told you, girlie. A
dear old friend of mine when I was a young man
— the best friend I ever had. Jim is named after
him."

"Is he dead now?"

Mr. Linton hesitated.

"We lost him years ago," he said sadly. "A great
trouble came upon him — he lost some money,
and was falsely accused of dishonesty, and he had
to go to prison. When he came out his wife refused
to see him; they had made her believe him a thief,
and she was a hard woman, although she loved
him. She sent a message that he must never try
to see her or their boy."

"She was cruel." Norah's eyes were angry.

"She was very unhappy, so we mustn't judge her," her father said, sighing. "Poor soul, she paid for her harshness. Later the truth of the whole bad business came out, and she would have given the world to be able to beg his forgiveness — only it was too late."

"Was he dead, Daddy?"

"They found his body in the river," said Mr. Linton. "Poor old chap, he couldn't stand the loss of his whole world. I've wished ever since that I could tell him I never believed the lie for a moment. I was in England at the time, and I knew nothing about it until he was dead."

"Poor old Daddy," said Norah softly.

"Oh, it's an old story, now," Mr. Linton said. "Only I never lost the regret — and the wish that I could have done something to help my old friend. I don't quite know why I've told you about it, except that I want you to be kind to young Dick Stephenson, because his life has been a sad enough one."

"Is his mother alive?"

"She lives in Melbourne," said her father. "I think she only lives for this boy, and the time when she can go to her husband and beg his forgiveness. He'll give it, too — poor old Jim. He could never bear malice in his life, and I'm certain death couldn't change his nature. The lad seems a good chap; he's had a first-rate education. But his mother never gave him any profession; I don't know why. Women aren't made for business. So he wants to teach."

"I'll be good to him, Daddy." Norah slipped her hand into her father's.

"That's my little girl. I knew I could depend on you," said Mr. Linton. A far-away look came into his eyes, and he pulled hard at his pipe. Norah guessed he was thinking of days of long ago.

She pulled her bait up, and examination told her it was untouched. The fish were certainly shy, and another half-hour's tempting did not bring them to the hook. It was exceedingly dull. Norah wound up her line slowly. She also had been thinking.

"I'm going for a walk, Daddy," she said.

"All right, dear; don't go far," said her father absently.

Norah walked soberly along the log until she reached the creek bank, and then jumped ashore. She looked round at her father, but he was absorbed in his fishing and his thoughts, and so the little girl slipped away into the bush. She made her way among the trees quickly, keeping to the line of the creek. Presently she sat down on a moss-grown stump and thought deeply.

The Hermit had been pretty constantly in Norah's mind since the troopers had been scouring the district in their search for the Winfield murderer. She had longed intensely to warn him — scenting certain unpleasantness to him, and possible danger, although she was loyally firm in the belief that he could not be the man for whom they were searching. Still, how like the description was! Even though Norah's faith was unshaken, she knew that the veriest hint of the Hermit's existence would bring the troopers down on him as fast as they could travel to his camp. She put aside resolutely the thoughts that flocked to her mind — the strange old man's lonely life, his desire to hide himself from his fellow-men.

"I don't understand it a bit," she said aloud. "But I'll have to tell him. He ought to know."

With that she sprang up and ran on through the scrub. It was thick enough to puzzle many a traveller, but the little maid of the bush saw no difficulties in the way. It was quite clear to her, remembering how the Hermit had guided their merry party on the first visit, weeks ago. At the exact spot on the creek she struck off at right angles into the heart of the trees, keeping a sharp lookout for the tall old form that might appear at any moment — hoping that her father might not grow tired of fishing and coo-ee for her to return.

But there was silence in the bush, and no sign of the Hermit could be seen. The thought came to Norah that he might have struck camp, and gone farther back into the wild country, away from the men he dreaded. But she put the idea from her. Somehow she felt that he was there.

She came to the clump of dogwood that hid the old log along which lay the last part of the track to the Hermit's camp and, climbing up, ran along it lightly. There were no recent footprints upon it. Suddenly the silence of the surroundings fell heavily on her heart.

Reaching the end of the log that gave access to the clearing, she took a hasty glance round. The ashes of the fire were long dead. No one was there.

Norah's heart thumped heavily. For a moment she fought with the longing to run back — back from this strange, silent place — back to Daddy. Then she gulped down something in her throat, and giving herself an impatient shake, she went resolutely across the clearing to the tent and peeped in.

The interior of the tent was as neat and home-like as when Norah had seen it first. The quaint bits of furniture stood in their places, and the skins lay on the floor. But Norah saw nothing but her friend's face.

The Hermit was lying on his bunk — a splendid old figure in his dress of soft furry skins, but with a certain helplessness about him that brought Norah's heart into her mouth. As the flap of the tent lifted he turned his head with difficulty, and looked at the little girl with weary, burning eyes that held no light of recognition. His face was ghastly white beneath the sunburnt skin, which was drawn like parchment over the cheekbones. A low moan came from his dry lips.

"Water!"

Norah cast a despairing glance around. An empty billy by the old man told its own tale, and a hurried search in the camp only revealed empty vessels.

"I'll be back in a minute," said Norah, sobbing.

Afterwards she could not remember how she had got down to the creek. Her blouse was torn, and there were long scratches on her wrists, and she was panting, as she came back to the sick man, and, struggling to raise his heavy head, held a cup to his lips. He drank fiercely, desperately, as Norah had seen starving cattle drink when released after a long journey in the trucks. Again

and again he drank — until Norah grew afraid
and begged him to lie down. He obeyed her meekly
and smiled a little, but there was no compre-
hension in the fevered eyes. She put her hand on
his forehead and started at its burning heat.

"Oh, what'll I do with you!" she said in her
perplexity.

"Do?" said the Hermit with startling suddenness. "But I'm dead!" He closed his eyes and
lay very still. "Dead — ages ago!" He muttered. A
second he lay so, and then he turned and looked
at her. "Where's the child?" he asked. "I must go
to him; let me go, I tell you." He tried to rise, but
fell back weakly. "Water!" he begged.

She gave him water again, and then bathed his
face and hands, using her handkerchief for a
sponge. He grew quieter, and once or twice Norah
thought he seemed to know her; but at the end he
closed his eyes and lay motionless.

"I'll be back very soon," she said. "Do please be
still, dear Mr. Hermit!" She bent over him and
kissed his forehead, and he stirred and murmured
a name she could not catch. Then he relapsed into
unconsciousness, and Norah turned and ran wildly
into the scrub.

To bring Daddy — Daddy, who knew
everything, who always understood! There was no
other thought in her mind now. Whatever the
Hermit might have done, he needed help now most
sorely — and Daddy was the only one would could
give it. Only the way seemed long as she raced
through the trees, seeing always that haggard,
pain-wrung face on the rude bunk. If only they
were in time!

Mr. Linton, sitting on the log and lazily watching his idle float, started at the voice that called to him from the bank; and at sight of the little girl he leaped to his feet and ran towards her.

"Norah! What is it?"

She told him, clutching to him and sobbing; tugging at him all the time to make him come quickly. A strange enough tale it seemed to Mr. Linton — of hermits and hidden camps, and the Winfield murderer, and someone who needed help — but there was that in Norah's face and in her unfamiliar emotion that made him hurry through the scrub beside her, although he did not understand what he was to find, and was only conscious of immense relief to know that she herself was safe, after the moment of terror that her first cry had given him.

Norah steadied herself with a great effort, as they came to the silent camp.

"He's there," she said, pointing.

Mr. Linton understood something then, and he went forward quickly. The hermit was still unconscious. His hollow eyes met them blankly as they entered the tent.

"Oh, he's ill, Daddy! Will he die?"

But David Linton did not answer. He was staring at the unconscious face before him, and his own was strangely white. As Norah looked at him, struck with a sudden wonder, her father fell on his knees and caught the sick man's hand.

"Jim!" he said, and a sob choked his voice. "Old chum — Jim!"

CHAPTER 15

For Friendship

DADDY!"

At the quivering voice her father lifted his head and Norah saw that his eyes were wet.

"It's my dear old friend Stephenson," he said brokenly. "I told you about him. We thought he was dead — there was the body; I don't understand, but this is he, and he's alive, thank God!"

The Hermit stirred and begged again for water, and Mr. Linton held him while he drank. His face grew anxious as he felt the scorching heat of the old man's body.

"He's so thirsty," Norah said tremulously, "goodness knows when he'd had a drink. His poor lips were all black and cracked when I found him."

"Had he no water near him?" asked her father, quickly. "You got this?"

"Yes, from the creek," Norah nodded. "I'll get some more, Daddy; the billy's nearly empty."

When Norah returned, laden with two cans, her father met her with a very grave face.

"That's my girl," he said, taking the water from her. "Norah, I'm afraid he's very ill. It looks uncommonly like typhoid."

"Will he — will he die, Daddy?"

"I can't tell, dear. What's bothering me is how to get help for him. He wants a doctor immediately — wants a dozen things I haven't got here. I wish that blessed black boy hadn't gone! I don't quite know what to do — I can't leave you here while I get help — he's half delirious now."

"You must let me go," said Norah quietly. "I can — easily."

"You!" said her father, looking down at the steady face. "That won't do, dear — not across fifteen miles of lonely country. I — " The Hermit cried out suddenly, and tried to rise, and Mr. Linton had to hold him down gently, but the struggle was a painful one, and when it was over the strong man's brow was wet. "Poor old chap!" he muttered brokenly.

Norah caught his arm.

"You see, I must go, Daddy," she said. "There's no one else — and he'll die! Truly I can, Daddy — quite well. Bobs'll look after me."

"Can you?" he said, looking down at her. "You're sure you know the track?"

"Course I can," said his daughter scornfully.

"I don't see anything for it," Mr. Linton said, an anxious frown knitting his brow. "His life hangs on getting help, and there's no other way. I'll have to risk you, my little girl."

"There's no risk," said Norah. "Don't you worry, Daddy, dear. Just tell me what you want."

Mr. Linton was writing hurriedly in his pocket-book.

"Send into Cunjee for Dr. Anderson as hard as a man can travel," he said shortly. "Don't wait for him, however; get Mrs. Brown to pack these things

from my medicine-chest, and let Billy get a fresh
horse and bring them back to me, and he needn't
be afraid of knocking his horse up. I'm afraid we're
too late as it is. Can he find his way here?"

"He's been here."

"That's all right, then. Tell Anderson I think it's
typhoid, and if he thinks we can move him, let
Wright follow the doctor out with the
express-wagon — Mrs. Brown will know what to
send to make it comfortable. Can you manage
Bobs?"

"Yes — of course."

Mr. Linton put his hand on her shoulder.

"I've got to let you go," he said. "It's the only
way. Remember, I won't have a minute's peace
until I know you've got safely home."

"I'll be all right, Daddy — true. And I'll hurry.
Don't bother about me."

"Bother!" he said. "My little wee mate." He
kissed her twice. "Now — hurry!"

Bobs, grazing peacefully under a big gum tree, was
startled by a little figure, staggering beneath
saddle and bridle. In a minute Norah was on his
back, and they were galloping across the plain
towards home.

A young man sat on the cap of the stockyard fence
at Billabong homestead, swinging his legs
listlessly and wishing for something to do. He
blessed the impulse that had brought him to the
station before his time, and wondered if things
were likely to be always as dull.

"Unless my small pupil stirs things up, I don't

fancy this life much," he said moodily, in which
he showed considerable impatience of judgment,
being but a young man.

Across the long, grey plain a tiny cloud
gathered, and the man watched it lazily.
Gradually it grew larger, until it resolved itself
into dust — and the dust into a horse and rider.

"Someone coming," he said, with faint interest.
"By Jove, it's a girl! She's racing, too. Wonder if
anything's wrong?"

He slipped from the fence and went forward to
open the gate, looking at the advancing pair. A
big bay pony, panting, and dripping with sweat,
but with "go" in him yet for a final spring; and on
his back a little girl, flushed and excited, with
tired, set lips. He expected her to stop at the gate,
but she flashed by him with a glance and a brief
"Thank you," galloping up to the gate of the yard.
Almost before the pony stopped she was out of the
saddle and running up the path to the kitchen.
The man saw Mrs. Brown come out, and heard
her cry of surprise as she caught the child to her.

"Something's up," said the stranger. He followed
at a run.

In the kitchen Norah was clinging to Mrs.
Brown, quivering with the effort not to cry.

"Someone ill in the bush?" said the astonished
Brownie, patting her nurseling. "Yes, Billy's here,
dearie — and all the horses are in. Where's the
note? I'll see to it. Poor pet! don't take on, lovey,
there. See, here's your new governess, Mr.
Stephenson.

Norah straightened with a gasp of astonishment.

"You!" she said.

"Me!" said Dick Stephenson ungrammatically, holding out his hand. "You're my pupil, aren't you? Is anything wrong?"

"There's a poor gentleman near to dyin' in the scrub," volunteered Mrs. Brown, "an' Miss Norah's come all the way in for help. Fifteen mile, if it's an inch! I don't know 'ow you did it, my blessed pet!"

"You don't mean to say you did!" said the new "governess" amazed. Small girls like this had not come his way. "By Jove, you're plucky! I say, what's up?"

Norah was very pale.

"Are you really Mr. Stephenson?" she asked. "I ... You'll be surprised ... He's ..." Her voice failed her.

"Don't worry to talk," he said gently. "You're done up."

"No — " She steadied her voice. "I must tell you. It's — it's — your father!"

Dick Stephenson's face suddenly darkened.

"I beg your pardon," he said stiffly. "You're making a mistake; my father is dead."

"He's not," said Norah. "He's my dear Hermit, and he's out there with typhoid, or some beastly thing. We found him — and Dad knows him quite well. It's really him. He never got drowned."

"Do you know what you're saying?" The man's face was white.

But Norah's self-command was at an end. She buried her face in Brownie's kind bosom, and burst into a passion of crying.

The old woman rocked her to and fro gently

until the sobs grew fainter, and Norah, shame-faced, began to feel for her handkerchief. Then Mrs. Brown put her into the big cushioned rocking-chair.

"Now, you must be brave and tell us, dearie," she said gently. "This is pretty wonderful for Mr. Stephenson."

So Norah, with many catchings of the breath, told them all about the Hermit, and of her father's recognition of him, saying only nothing of her long and lonely ride. Before she had finished Billy was on the road to Cunjee, flying for the doctor. Dick Stephenson, white-faced, broke in on the story.

"How can I get out there?" he asked shortly.

"I'll take you," Norah said.

"You! — that's out of the question."

"No, it isn't. I'm not tired," said Norah, quite unconscious of saying anything but the truth. "I knew I'd have to, anyhow, because only Billy and I know the way to the Hermit's camp, and he has to fetch the doctor. You tell Wright to get Banker for you, and put my saddle on Jim's pony — and to look well after Bobs. Hurry, while Brownie gets the other things."

Dick Stephenson made no further protests, his brain awhirl as he raced to the stables. Brownie protested certainly, but did her small maid's bidding the while. But it was a very troubled old face that looked long after the man and the little girl, as they started on the long ride back to the camp.

Mile after mile they swung across the grey plain.

Norah did not try to talk. She disdained the idea

that she was tired, but a vague feeling told her
that she must save all her energies to guide the
way back to the camp hidden in the scrub, where
the Hermit lay raving, and her father sat beside
the lonely bed.

Neither was her companion talkative. He stared
ahead, as if trying to pierce with his eyes the line
of timber that blurred across the landscape. Norah
was glad he did not bother her with questions. She
had told him all she knew, and now he was
content to wait.

"It must be hard on him, all the same," thought
Norah, looking at the set young face, and sparing
an instant to approve of the easy seat in the saddle
displayed by her new "governess". "To believe that
your father was dead all these years, and then
suddenly to find him alive — but how far apart
in every way! Why, you hardly know," mused
Norah, "whether you'll like him — whether he'll
be glad to see you! Not that anyone could fail to
like the Hermit — anyone with sense, that is!"

Mile after mile! The plain slipped away beneath
the even beat of the steadily cantering hoofs. The
creek, forded slowly, sank into the distance behind
them; before, the line of timber grew darker and
more definite. Jim's pony was not far inferior to
Bobs in pace and easiness, and his swinging canter
required no effort to sit, but a great weariness
began to steal over his rider. Dick Stephenson,
glancing at her frequently, saw the pallor creeping
upon the brave little face.

He pulled up.

"We'll go steady for a while," he said. "No good
knocking you up altogether."

Norah checked her pony unwillingly.

"Oh, don't you think we ought to hurry?" she said. "Dad's waiting for those medicines you've got, you know."

"Yes, I know. But I don't think we'll gain much by overdoing it."

"If you're thinking about me," Norah said impatiently, "you needn't. I'm as right as rain. You must think I'm pretty soft. Do come on!"

He looked at her steadily. Dark shadows of weariness lay under the brave eyes that met his.

"Why, no," he said. "Fact is, I'm a bit of a new chum myself where riding's concerned — you mustn't be too ashamed of me. I think we'd better walk for a while. And you take this."

He poured something from his flask into its little silver cup and handed it to Norah. Their eyes met, and she read his meaning through the kindness of the words that cloaked what he felt. Above her weariness a sense of comfort stole over Norah. She knew in that look that henceforth they were friends.

She gulped down the drink, which was hateful, but presently sent a feeling of renewed strength through her tired limbs. They rode on in silence for some time, the horses brushing through the long soft grass. Dick Stephenson pulled hard at his pipe.

"Did — did my father know you this morning?" he asked suddenly.

Norah shook her head mournfully.

"He didn't know anyone," she answered, "only asked for water and said things I couldn't under-stand. Then when Dad came, he knew him at once,

but the Hermit didn't even seem to know that Dad
was there."

"Did he look very bad?"

"Yes — pretty bad," said Norah, hating to hurt
him. "He was terribly flushed, and, oh! his poor
eyes were awful, so burning and sunken. And —
oh! — let's canter, Mr. Stephenson, please!"

This time there was no objection. Banker
jumped at the quick touch of the spur as
Stephenson's heel went home. Side by side they
cantered steadily until Norah pulled her pony in
at length at the entrance to the timber, where the
creek swung into Anglers' Bend.

"We're nearly there," she said.

But to the man watching in the Hermit's camp
the hours were long indeed.

The Hermit was too weak to struggle much.
There had been a few sharp paroxysms of
delirium, such as Norah had seen, during which
David Linton had been forced to hold the old man
down with unwilling force. But the struggles soon
brought their own result of helpless weakness, and
the Hermit subsided into restless unconsciousness,
broken by feeble mutterings, of which few coherent
words could be caught. "Dick" was frequently on
the fevered lips. Once he smiled suddenly, and Mr.
Linton, bending down, heard a faint whisper of
"Norah".

Sitting beside his old friend in the lonely silence
of the bush, he studied the ravages time and
sorrow had wrought in the features he knew.
Greatly changed as Jim Stephenson was, his face
lined and sunken, and his beard long and white
as snow, it was still, to David Linton, the friend

of his boyhood come back from the grave and from his burden of unmerited disgrace. The frank blue eyes were as brave as ever; they met his with no light of recognition, but with their clear gaze undimmed. A sob rose in the strong man's throat — if he could but see again that welcoming light! — hear once more his name on his friend's lips! If he were not too late!

The Hermit muttered and tossed on his narrow bed. The watcher's thoughts fled to the little messenger galloping over the long miles of lonely country — his little motherless girl, whom he had sent on a mission that might so easily spell disaster. Horrible thoughts came into the father's mind. He pictured Bobs putting his hoof into a hidden crab-hole — falling — Norah lying white and motionless, perhaps far from the track. That was not the only danger. Bad characters were to be met with in the bush and the pony was valuable enough to tempt a desperate man — such as the Winfield murderer — who was roaming the district, nobody knew where. There was a score of possible risks; to battle with them, a little maid of twelve, strong only in the self-reliance bred of the bush. The father looked at the ghastly face before him, and asked himself questions that tortured — Was it right to have let the young life go to save the old one that seemed just flickering out? He put his face in his hands and groaned.

How long the hours were! He calculated fever-ishly the time it would take the little messenger to reach home if all went well; then how long it must be before a man could come out to him.. At that thought he realized for the first time the difficulty Norah had seen in silence — who should come out to him? Billy must fetch the doctor and guide him to the sick man; but no one else save Norah herself knew the track to the little camp, hidden so cunningly in the scrub. At that rate it might be many hours before he knew if his child were safe. Anxiety for the remedies for his friend was swallowed up in the anguish of uncertainty for Norah. It seemed to him that he must go to seek her — that he could not wait! He started up, but, as if alarmed by his sudden movement, the Hermit cried out and tried to rise, struggling feebly with the strong hands that were quick to hold him back. When the struggle was over David Linton sat down again. How could he leave him?

Then across his agony of uncertainty came a clear childish voice. The tent flaps were parted and Norah stood in the entrance white and trembling, but with a glad smile of welcome on her lips — behind her a tall man, who trembled, too. David Linton did not see him. All the world seemed whirling round him as he caught his child in his arms.

CHAPTER 16

Fighting Death

Y OU!" Mr. Linton said.

He had put Norah gently into the rough chair, and turned to Dick Stephenson, who was standing by his father, his lips twitching. They gripped hands silently.

"You can recognise him?"

"I'd know him anywhere," the son said. "Poor old dad! You think —?"

"I don't know," the other said hastily. "Can't tell until Anderson comes. But I fancy it's typhoid. You brought the things? Ah!" His eyes brightened as they fell on the leather medicine-case Mrs. Brown had sent, and in a moment he was unstrapping it with quick, nervous fingers.

The Hermit stirred, and gasped for water. He drank readily enough from the glass Mr. Linton held to his lips, while his son supported him with strong young arms. There was not much they could do.

"Anderson should be here before long," Mr. Linton said. "What time did Billy leave?"

"A little after twelve."

"What did he ride?"

"A big black."

"That's right," Mr. Linton nodded. "Anderson

would motor out to Billabong, I expect, and Mrs. Brown would have the fresh horses ready. They should not be very long, with ordinary luck. Billy left about twelve, did he? By Jove, Norah must have made great time! It was after half-past ten when she left me."

"She and the pony looked as if they'd done enough."

"And she came back! I hadn't realised it all in the minute of seeing her," her father said, staring at Stephenson. "Norah, dear, are you quite knocked up?" He turned to speak, but broke off sharply. Norah was gone.

Mr. Linton turned on his heel without a word, and hurried out of the tent, with Stephenson at his side. Just for a moment the Hermit was forgotten in the sudden pang of anxiety that gripped them both. In the open they glanced round quickly, and a sharp exclamation of dismay broke from the father.

Norah was lying in a crumpled heap under a tree. There was something terribly helpless in the little, quiet figure, face downwards, on the grass.

Just for a moment, as he fell on his knees beside her, David Linton lost his self-control. He called her piteously, catching the limp body to him. Dick Stephenson's hand fell on his shoulder.

"She's only fainted," he said huskily. "Over-tired, that's all. Put her down, sir, please" — and Mr. Linton, still trembling, laid the little girl on the grass, and loosened her collar, while the other forced a few drops from his flask between the pale lips.

Gradually Norah's eyes flickered and opened, and colour crept into her cheeks.

"Daddy!" she whispered.

"Don't walk, my darling," her father said. "Lie still."

"I'm all right now," Norah said presently. "I'm so sorry I frightened you, Daddy — I couldn't help it."

"You should have kept still, dear," said her father. "Why did you go out?"

"I felt rummy," said his daughter inelegantly, "a queer, whirly-go-round feeling. I guessed I must be going to tumble over. It didn't seem any good making a duffer of myself when you were busy with the Hermit, so I cut out."

Dick Stephenson turned sharply and, without a word, strode back into the tent.

Norah turned with a sudden movement to her father, clinging to the rough serge of his coat. Something like a tear fell on her upturned face as the strong arms enfolded her.

"Why — Daddy — dear old Dad!" she whispered.

It was nearly twilight when Dr. Anderson and Billy rode into the clearing, to the joy of the anxious watchers.

The doctor did not waste any words. He slipped off his horse and entered the tent. Presently Dick Stephenson came out and sat down beside Norah to await the verdict.

"I can't do any good there," he said, "and there's no room."

Norah nodded. Just then there seemed nothing to say to this son whose father, so lately given back from the grave, seemed to be slipping away again without a word. She slid her hand into his and felt his fingers close warmly upon it.

"I can stand it," he said brokenly, after a little, "if he can only know we — the world — knows he was never guilty — if I can only tell him that. I can't bear him to die not knowing that."

"He'd know it anyhow."

The little voice was very low, but the lad heard it.

"I — I guess he will," he said, "and that's better. But I would like to make it up to him a bit — while he's here."

Then they were silent. The shadows deepened across the clearing. Long since the sun had disappeared behind the rim of encircling trees.

The tent flaps parted and the doctor and Mr. Linton came out. Dick rose and faced them. He could not utter the question that trembled on his lips.

The doctor nodded cheerily.

"Well, Norah?" he said. "Yes; I think we'll pull the patient through this time, Mr. Stephenson. It'll be a fight, for he's old and weakened by exposure and lack of proper food, but I think we'll do it." He talked on hopefully appearing not to see the question the son could not altogether hide. "Take him home? Yes, we'll get him home tomorrow, I think. We can't nurse him out here. The express-wagon's following with all sorts of comforting things. Trust your Old Mrs. Brown for that, Norah. Most capable woman! Mattresses, air pillows, nourishment — she'd thought of everything, and the wagon was all ready to start when I got to Billabong. By the way, Billy was to go back to show Wright the way. Where are you, Billy? Why haven't you gone?"

"Plenty!" said Billy hastily, as he disappeared.

"I hear you've been flying all over the country, Norah," said Dr. Anderson, lighting a cigarette. "What do you mean by looking so white?"

The tale of Norah's iniquities was unfolded to him, and the doctor felt her pulse in a friendly way.

"You'll have to go to bed soon," he said. "Can't have you knocking yourself up, you know; and we've got to make an early start tomorrow to avoid the worst heat of the day for the patient. Also, you will take a small tabloid to make you 'buck up,' if you know what that means, Norah!" Norah grinned. "Ah, well, Mr. Stephenson here will make you forget all that undesirable knowledge before long — lost in a maze of Euclid, and Latin, and Greek, and trigonometry, and things!"

"I say!" gasped Norah.

"Well, you may," grinned the doctor. "I foresee lively times for you and your tutor in the paths of learning, young lady. First of all, however, you'll have to under-nurse to our friend the patient, with Mrs. Brown as head. And that reminds me — someone must sit up tonight."

"That's my privilege," said Dick Stephenson quickly.

And all that night, after the camp had quietened to sleep, the son sat beside his newly found father, watching in the silver moonlight every change that flitted across the wan old face. The Hermit had not yet recovered consciousness, but under the doctor's remedies he had lost the terrible restlessness of delirium and lay for the most part calmly. In heart, as he watched him, Dick was but a little boy again, loving above all the world the tall "Daddy" who was his hero — longing with all the little boy's devotion and all the strength of his manhood to make up to him for the years he had suffered alone.

But the calm face on the bed never showed sign of recognition. Once or twice the Hermit muttered, and his boy's name was on his lips. The pulse fluttered feebly. The great river flowed very close about his feet.

CHAPTER 17

The End of the Struggle

THE long slow journey to Billabong homestead was accomplished.

The Hermit had never regained consciousness throughout the weary hours during which every jolt of the express-wagon over the rough tracks had sent a throb to the hearts of the watchers. All unconscious he had lain while they lifted him from the bunk where he had slept for so many lonely nights. The men packed his few personal belongings quickly. Norah, remembering a hint dropped by the Hermit in other days, had instituted a search for buried papers, which resulted in the unearthing of a tin box containing various documents. She had insisted, too, that the rough furniture should go, and it was piled in the front of the wagon. Another man had brought out the old pack mare for the baggage of the original fishing party, and the whole cavalcade moved off before the sun had got above the horizon.

But it was a tedious journey. Dr. Anderson sat beside his patient, watching the feeble action of the heart and the flickering pulse, plying him with stimulants and nourishment, occasionally calling a halt for a few minutes' complete rest. Close to the wheel Dick Stephenson rode, his eyes scarcely leaving his father's face. On the other side, Norah and her father rode in silent, miserable anxiety, fretting at their utter helplessness. Dr. Anderson glanced sharply now and then at the little girl's face.

"This isn't good for her," he said at length quietly to Mr. Linton. "She's had too much already. Take her home." He raised his voice. "You'd better go on," he said, "let Mrs. Brown know just what is coming; she'll need you to help her prepare the patient's room, Norah. You, too, Stephenson."

Dick shook his head.

"I won't leave him, thanks," he said. "I'd rather not — he might become conscious."

"No chance of that," the doctor said. "Best not, too, until we have him safely in bed. However, stay if you like — perhaps it's as well. I think, Linton, you'd better send a wire to Melbourne for a trained nurse."

"And one to mother," Dick said quickly.

"That's gone already," Mr. Linton said. "I sent George back with it last night when he brought the mare out." He smiled in answer to Dick's grateful look. "Well, come on, Norah."

The remembrance of that helpless form in the bottom of the wagon haunted Norah's memory all through the remainder of the ride home. She was thoroughly tired now — the excitement that had kept her up the day before had prevented her from sleeping, and she scarcely could keep upright in the saddle. However, she set her teeth to show no sign of weakness that should alarm her father, and endeavoured to have a smile for him whenever his anxious gaze swept her white face.

The relief of seeing the red roof of home! That last mile was the longest of all — and when at length they were at the gate, and she had climbed stiffly off her pony, she could only lean against his shoulder and shake from heat to foot. Mr. Linton picked her up bodily and carried her, feebly protesting, into Mrs. Brown.

"Only knocked up," he said, in answer to the old woman's terrified exclamation. "Bed is all she needs — and hot soup, if you've got it. Norah, dear" — as she begged to be allowed to remain and help — "you can do nothing just now, except get yourself all right. Do as I tell you, girlie"; and in an astonishingly short space of time Norah found herself tucked up in bed in her darkened room, with Daddy's hand fast in hers, and a comforting feeling of everything fading away to darkness and sleep.

It was twilight when she opened her eyes again, and Brownie sat knitting by her side.

"Bless your dear heart," she said fervently. "Yes, the old gentleman's come, an' he's quite comferable in bed — though he don't know no one yet. Dr. Anderson's gone to Cunjee, but he's coming back in his steam engine to stay all night; an' your pa's having his dinner, which he needs, poor man. An' he don't want you to get up, lovey, for there ain't nothin' you can do. I'll go and get you something to eat."

But it was Mr. Linton who came presently,

bearing a tray with dainty chicken and salad, and a glass of clear golden jelly. He sat by Norah while she ate.

"We're pretty anxious, dear," he told her, when she had finished, and was snugly lying down again, astonishingly glad of her soft bed. "You won't mind my not staying. I must be near old Jim. I'll be glad when Anderson's back. Try to go to sleep quickly." He bent to kiss her. "You don't know what a comfort your sleep has been to me, my girlie," he said. "Goodnight!"

It was the third day of the struggle with death over the Hermit's unconscious body, and again twilight was falling upon Billabong.

The house was hushed and silent. No footfall was allowed to sound where the echo might penetrate to the sick-room. Near its precincts Mrs. Brown and the Melbourne trained nurse reigned supreme, and Dr. Anderson came and went as often as he could manage the fourteen-mile spin out from Cunjee in his motor.

Norah had a new care — a little fragile old lady, with snowy hair, and depths of infinite sadness in her eyes, whom Dick Stephenson called "mother." The doctor would not allow either mother or son into the sick-room — the shock of recognition, should the Hermit regain consciousness suddenly, might be too much. So they waited about, agonisingly anxious, pitifully helpless. Dick rebelled against the idleness at length. It would kill him, he said, and, borrowing a spade from the Chinese gardener, he spent his time in heavy digging, within easy call of the house. But for the wife and mother there was no help. She was gently courteous to all, gently appreciative of Norah's attempts to occupy her thoughts. But throughout it all — whether she looked at the pets outside, or walked among the autumn roses in the garden, or struggled to eat at the table — she was listening, ever listening.

In the evening of the third day Mr. Linton came quickly into the drawing-room. Tears were falling down his face. He went up to Mrs. Stephenson and put his hand on her shoulder.

"It's — it's all right, we think," he said brokenly. "He's conscious and knew me, dear old chap! I was sitting by the bed, and suddenly his eyes opened and all the fever had gone. 'Why, Davy!' he said. I told him everything was all right, and he mustn't talk — and he's taken some nourishment, and gone off into a natural sleep. Anderson's delighted." Then he caught Mrs. Stephenson quickly as she slipped to his feet, unconscious.

Then there were days of dreary waiting, of slow, harassing convalescence. The patient did not seem to be alive to any outside thought. He gained strength very slowly, but he lay always silent, asking no questions, only when Mr. Linton entered the room showing any sign of interest. The doctor was vaguely puzzled, vaguely anxious.

"Do you think I could go and see him?" Norah was outside the door of the sick-room. The doctor often found her there — a little silent figure, listening vainly for her friend's voice. She looked up pleadingly. "Not if you think I oughtn't to," she said.

"I don't believe it would hurt him," Dr.

Anderson said, looking down at her. "Might wake him up a bit — I know you won't excite him."

So it was that the Hermit, waking from a restless sleep, found by his side a small person with brown curls that he remembered.

"Why, it's my little friend," he murmured, feeling weakly for her hand. "This seems a queer world — old friends and new, all mixed up."

"I'm so glad you're better, dear Mr. Hermit," Norah said. She bent and kissed him. "And we're all friends — everybody."

"You did that once before," he said feebly. "No one had kissed me for such a long, long while. But I mustn't let you."

"Why?" asked Norah blankly.

"Because — because people don't think much of me, Miss Norah," he said, a deep shade falling on his fine old face. "They say I'm no good. I don't suppose I'd be allowed to be here, only I'm an old man, and I'm going to die."

"But you're not!" Norah cried. "Dr. Anderson says you're new! and — and — oh, you're making a great mistake. Everyone wants you."

"Me!" said the Hermit, in sudden bitter scorn. "No, only strangers like you. Not my own."

"Oh, you don't know," Norah protested. She was painfully aware of the order not to excite the patient, but it was awful to let him be so unhappy! "Dad's not a stranger — he always knew you. And see how he wants you!"

"Dad?" the Hermit questioned feebly. "Is David Linton your father?" She nodded, and for a minute he was silent. "No wonder you and I were friends!"

he said. "But you're not all — not even you and Davy."

"No, but —"

He forced a smile, in pity for her perplexity.

"Dear little girl, you don't understand," he said. "There's something even friendship can't wipe out, though such friendship as your father's can bridge it over. But it's always there — a black, cruel gulf. And that's disgrace!"

Norah could not bear the misery of his eyes.

"But if it's all a horrible mistake?" she said. "If everybody knew it —?"

"If it's a mistake!"

The Hermit's hand was on her wrist like a vice. For a moment Norah shivered in fear of what her words might have done.

"What do you mean? For God's sake, tell me!"

She steadied her voice to answer him bravely.

"Please, you mustn't get excited, dear Mr. Hermit," she said. "I'll tell you. Dad told me all about it before we found you. It's all a terrible mistake. Everyone knows you were a good man. Everyone wants to be friends with you. Only they thought you were dead."

"I managed that." His voice was sharp and eager. "I saw the other body in the river and the rest was easy." He struggled for calmness and Norah held a glass of water to his lips.

"Please don't get excited!" she begged.

"I won't," he smiled at her. "Tell me — does everyone know?"

"Everyone," Norah nodded. There was a step behind her and a sudden light flashed into the Hermit's eyes.

"Davy! is it true? I am cleared?"

"Years ago, old man." David Linton's voice was husky. "All the world wants to make it up to you."

"All the world — they're only two!" the sick man said. "Do they know?"

"Yes."

"Where are they?"

For a moment Mr. Linton hesitated, not knowing what risk he might run.

"Oh! for pity's sake don't be cautious, David," the Hermit begged. "I'll be calm — anything — only don't refuse a starving man bread! Davy, tell me!"

"They're here, old man."

"Here! Can I — will they —?"

"Ah, we've got to be careful of you, Jim, old chap," Mr. Linton said. "You've been a very sick man — and you're not better yet. But they're only living on the hope of seeing you — of having you again — of making it up to you."

"And they believe in me?"

"The boy — Dick — never believed a word against you," Mr. Linton said. "And your wife — ah, if she doubted, she has paid for it again and again in tears. You'll forgive her, Jim?"

"Yes," he said simply. "I've been bitter enough. God knows, but it all seems gone. You'll bring her, Davy?"

But at the word Norah was out of the room, racing along the hall.

Out in the gardens Dick Stephenson dug mightily in the hard soil, and his mother watched him, listening always. She heard the flying

footsteps on the gravel and turned quickly to meet
Norah.

"Mrs. Stephenson, he wants you!"

"Is he worse?" Dick gasped.

"No — I think he's all right. But he knows
everything and he wants you both!" In his room
the Hermit heard the steps in the hall — the light,
slow feet, and the man's tread, that curbed its
impatience, lingering to support them. His breath
came quickly as he stared at the door.

Then for a moment they faced each other, after
the weary years; each gaunt and wan and old, but
in their eyes the light and the love of long ago.
The Hermit's eyes wandered an instant to his son's
face, seeking in the stalwart man the little lad he
knew. Then they came back to his wife.

"Mary!"

"Jim!" She tottered to the bed.

"Jim — can you forgive me?"

"Forgive — oh, my girl!" The two grey heads
were close together. David Linton slipped from the
room.

CHAPTER 18

Evening

THEY were all sitting on the lawn in the twilight. Norah had dispensed afternoon tea with laborious energy, ably seconded by Dick, who carried cups and cake, and made himself generally useful. Then they had talked until the sun slipped over the edge of the plain. There was so much to talk of in those days.

The Hermit had been allowed to leave his room a fortnight since. He was still weak, but strength was coming every day — strength that follows on happiness. Norah declared he grew better every day and no one contradicted her.

He and his wife sat hand in hand. They were rarely seen any other way — perfect content on each placid face. Dick lay on the grass at their feet and smoked, and threw stems of buffalo grass at Norah, who returned them honourably. Mr. Linton, also smoking, surveyed the group with satisfaction.

They had been talking over plans for the future, plans which Mr. Linton's masterfulness modified very considerably.

"Go away?" he said. "Certainly not! I've engaged your son as tutor to my daughter, and I really can't spare him from the poor neglected child!

Then, as you, curiously enough, don't wish to leave your son, the course is quite clear — you must stay here."

"I'm not going to live on you, Davy."

"You needn't. I'm bitterly in need of someone with a head for figures — a thing I never possessed. You can help me tremendously. And, good as dear old Brownie is, I know Norah ought to be with a gentlewoman — to learn the things that aren't in school books. It's the best chance you and I have ever had, isn't it, Norah? We aren't going to let it — or you — slip through our hands."

"It's — it's all very well, Davy, old man —"

"I know it is. Now, can't you let well alone, Jim? Talk of it again in five years' time — you may have better luck then. I don't say you will — but you may! Hang it all, man, you're not going to thwart me when I've just got my family together!"

"Well, I won't for a while," the Hermit said — and immediately received a kiss on the top of his head.

"Thank you, Norah," he said meekly.

"Don't mention it," Norah answered politely. "Oh, I'm so glad you're going to stay with us, Mr. Hermit!"

Norah had flatly declined to call her friend anything but the name she had given him in the bush. As for the Hermit, he was perfectly content with anything Norah did and had no idea of objecting.

"You heard, didn't you, Norah, that they'd found your friend, the Winfield murderer?" Mr. Linton asked.

"Daddy! — no!"

"Found his body in an old shaft — not far from Winfield. He had the stolen property on him, so there's no doubt of his guilt. So that clears your Hermit, even in your suspicious mind!"

"Ah, don't Daddy," Norah said, flushing. "I wasn't suspicious. I was a duffer."

"I don't think you were," the Hermit said decidedly. "A very sensible duffer, anyhow."

Dick laughed.

"No use trying to come between those two," he said.

"Not a bit," said the Hermit with great cheerfulness. He smiled at Norah. "You brought me back to life — twice."

"When I think — but for Norah," Mrs. Stephenson murmured brokenly, "no one would have known you were dying in that dreadful tent."

"Yes," said the Hermit, "but I didn't know anything about it. My best memory is of my little friend who brought me good news when I was wishing with all my soul that I'd died in the tent!"

"Don't, Jim!" said Mr. Linton.

"Well, between one and another there's a fair chance of spoiling my pupil," laughed Dick, stretching himself. "I'll have to be doubly stern to counteract the evil influences, Norah. You can prepare for awful times. When next Monday comes, Mr. Linton — may it be soon! — you can say goodbye to your pickle of a daughter. She will come out from my mill ground into the most approved type of young lady — accomplishments, prunes and prisms personified!"

Mr. Linton laughed.

"Will she?" he said, pulling Norah's hair gently.

"I wonder! Well, you can do your worst, Dick. Somehow, I fancy that under all the varnish I'll find my little bush maid."

Afterword

A Little Bush Maid was originally published in
1910. Norah, Jim, Wally and the other characters
at Billabong come to life as vividly now as they
did for teenage readers then; but because there
have been so many changes in our Australian way
of life, as well as in the rest of the world, since
that time, certain elements in the story may strike
today's readers as unfamiliar and sometimes
rather strange.

These changes relate in part to such matters as
transport, communications, scientific knowledge
and house and garden chores in the days before
washing machines or powered mowers, as well as
the sort of clothes people used to wear, compared
to our casual world of jeans and thongs. Norah is
thought to be quite daring because she wears a
divided skirt and sits astride her horse, instead of
wearing a long skirt and riding side-saddle.

In 1910, air travel had just begun; that year
was the trial flight of the first aeroplane to be
designed and built in Australia. People began to
think of airmail services between Australia and
the rest of the world, as well as other Australian
states, instead of waiting weeks for mail carried
by ship. Horse-drawn vehicles made up most of

the road traffic in town and country. Mr Linton doesn't possess a motor car, and the mustering at Billabong is carried out on horseback instead of motor-bike. Dr Anderson has a motor — Brownie refers to it as his "steam engine".

There were no radios, cassette players or tv, but (silent) movie films had arrived: in 1910 two Australian films were in production — *The Squatter's Daughter* and *The Life and Adventures of John Vane, Bushranger*. You could have listened to music on a phonograph (very scratchy and unsatisfactory in contrast to our world of stereo sound) and heard the latest pop hit — the tango. There's no phonograph at Billabong; instead, Norah plays the piano. Nor is there a telephone. Although the first telephone exchange opened in Melbourne in 1880, and the Sydney-Melbourne trunk line was in operation by 1907, private telephones were still quite rare, especially in the country. Mr Linton sends and receives urgent messages by telegram.

Other changes which have taken place relate to the ideas, opinions and attitudes people held then, compared to the way society in general thinks today. In 1910, in France, Marie Curie succeeded in isolating radium from its chloride — the first step in the study of radium physics, which led to vital developments in medicine and surgery. Mme Curie encountered a good deal of opposition within the male-dominated scientific world. At that time, women in Australia had only recently been given the right to vote in parliamentary elections. (As yet they were allowed to stand for election only to Federal Parliament and in South Australia.) It was unusual for them to enter the professions. Mostly, they stayed at home to look after their families and carry out "home duties". There's a hint of what we now call male chauvinism when Mr Linton declares at one point: "Women aren't meant for business" — yet he encourages Norah to help with mustering, as her pioneer grandmother did.

David Linton belongs to what was known as the "squattocracy", in the days when Australia was said to "ride on the sheep's back", meaning that most of the nation's prosperity was derived from rural industry. Jim will inherit from his father, but he says: "When I leave school I've got to work and earn my own living", an attitude that not every son of a rich father would have taken then. People were conscious of belonging to different levels of society, and more willing to conform to set patterns of behaviour. The servants at Billabong respectfully refer to their employer's son and daughter as "Mr Jim" and "Miss Norah". And, while Mr Linton respects Mrs Brown for the loving care she gives Norah, and the household skills she teaches her, he is glad when Mrs Stephenson comes to stay, because she is "a gentlewoman" who will be able to teach Norah "the things that aren't in the schoolbooks."

The attitude of the white people in the story towards Billy, the Aboriginal stable-hand, reflects the opinion genuinely held at that time by white Australians, that the Aborigines were a "dying race", to be patronised and paternalised during the final stages of their existence. Black Australians were thought of as being inferior to white

Australians. Colour prejudice was further shown in the "White Australia" policy of the day, which decreed that only white people (mainly from Britain) should be allowed to immigrate and increase the population — then approximately four and a half million. (The first official census was taken in 1911.) The underlying reason for this policy was that Australian workers feared an influx of cheap labour. Lee Wing, the Chinese gardener, possibly had a forbear who came to Australia during the gold rush, when large numbers of Chinese arrived to seek a fortune.

In 1910, Federation in Australia was just ten years old. A Labor government was in power and Andrew Fisher was Prime Minister.

With hindsight, we may disclaim many of the ideas, opinions and attitudes of 1910, and a few paragraphs which might be thought of as racist today have been omitted from the text. But it would be profitless to criticise the author of a story written at that time for relaying the attitudes of her day through her characters.

BARBARA KER WILSON

MARY GRANT BRUCE

Born in 1878, Mary Grant Bruce grew up in the Gippsland district of Victoria, near Sale.

Much of Mary's childhood was spent on the station of her grandparents which set the scene for her Billabong books. She loved riding and stock work and scorned the girlish pursuits of sewing and cooking. She was also a keen reader, and at seven had already begun writing poetry.

Her career as a published writer began as editor of the children's page of the Leader, *published by the* Age *newspaper. This was where* A Little Bush Maid *first appeared as a serial.*

In 1913 Mary travelled to London and met George Bruce. They returned to Australia to marry, but George, a British army major, was almost immediately recalled to his regiment in England. Their journey back to England by ship inspired From Billabong to London.

The couple made their home in Ireland and had two sons, Jonathan and Patrick. Patrick was tragically killed in 1927 when he accidentally shot himself, a repeat accident of Mary's childhood when her brother, Patrick, died in a similar shooting accident. Mary Grant Bruce died in 1958.

TITLES BY MARY GRANT BRUCE

A Little Bush Maid
Mates at Billabong
Norah of Billabong
From Billabong to London
Jim and Wally
Captain Jim
Back to Billabong
Billabong's Daughter
Billabong Adventurers
Bill of Billabong
Billabong's Luck
Wings Above Billabong
Billabong Gold
Son of Billabong
Billabong Riders